ONE

Jim Qwilleran prepared his bachelor breakfast with a look of boredom and distaste, accentuated by the down-curve of his bushy moustache. Using hot water from the tap, he made a cup of instant coffee with brown lumps floating on the surface. He dredged a doughnut from a crumb-filled canister that was beginning to smell musty. Then he spread a paper napkin on a table in a side window where the urban sun, filtered through smog, emphasized the bleakness of the furnished apartment.

Here Qwilleran ate his breakfast without tasting it, and considered his four problems:

At the moment he was womanless. He had received an eviction notice, and in three weeks he would be homeless. At the rate the moths were feeding on his neckwear, he would soon be tieless. And if he said the wrong thing to the managing editor today, he might very well be jobless. Over forty-five and jobless. It was not a cheerful prospect.

Fortunately, he was not friendless. On his breakfast table—along with a large unabridged dictionary, a stack of paperback books, a pipe rack with a single pipe, and a can of tobacco—there was a Siamese cat.

Qwilleran scratched his friend behind the ears, and said, "I'll bet you weren't allowed to sit on the breakfast table when you lived upstairs."

The cat, whose name was Koko, gave a satisfied wiggle, tilted his whiskers upward, and said, "YOW!"

He had lived with the newsman for six months, following the unfortunate demise of the man on the second floor. Qwilleran fed him well, conversed sensibly, and invented games to play—unusual pastimes that appealed to the cat's extraordinary intelligence.

Every morning Koko occupied one small corner of the breakfast table, arranging himself in a compact bundle, brown feet and tail tucked fastidiously under his white-breasted fawn body. In the mild sunshine Koko's slanted eyes were a brilliant blue, and his silky fur, like the newly spun spider web that spanned the window, glistened with a rainbow of iridescence.

"You make this apartment look like a dump," Qwilleran told him.

Koko squeezed his eyes and breathed faster. With each breath his nose changed from black velvet to black satin, then back to velvet.

Qwilleran lapsed again into deep thought, absently running a spoon handle through his moustache. This was the day he had promised himself to confront the managing editor and request a change of assignment. It was a risky move. The *Daily Fluxion* was known as a tight ship. Percy preached teamwork, team spirit, team discipline. Shoulder to shoulder, play the game, one for all. Ours not to question why. A long pull, a strong pull, a pull all together. We happy few!

"It's like this," Qwilleran told the cat. "If I walk into Percy's office and flatly request a change of assignment, I'm apt to land out in the street. That's the way he operates. And I can't afford to be unemployed—not right now—not till I build up a cash reserve."

Koko was listening to every word.

"If the worst came to the worst, I suppose I could get a job at the *Morning Rampage,* but I'd hate to work for that stuffy sheet."

Koko's eyes were large and full of understanding. "Yow," he said softly.

"I wish I could have a heart-to-heart talk with Percy, but it's impossible to get through to him. He's programmed, like a computer. His smile—very sincere. His handshake—very strong. His compliments—very gratifying. Then the next time you meet him on the elevator, he doesn't know you. You're not on his schedule for the day."

Koko shifted his position uneasily.

"He doesn't even look like a managing editor. He dresses like an advertising man. Makes me feel like a slob." Qwilleran passed a hand over the back of his neck. "Guess I should get a haircut."

Koko gurgled something in his throat, and Qwilleran recognized the cue. "Okay, we'll play the game. But only a few innings this morning. I've got to go to work."

He opened the big dictionary, which was remarkable for its tattered condition, and he and Koko played their word game. The way it worked, the cat dug his claws into the pages, and Qwilleran opened the books where he indicated, reading aloud the catchwords—the two boldface entries at the top of the columns. He read the right-hand page if Koko used his right paw, but usually it was the left-hand page. Koko was inclined to be a southpaw.

"*Design* and *desk*," Qwilleran read. "Those are easy. Score two points for me. . . . Go ahead, try again."

Koko cocked his brown ears forward and dug in with his claws.

"*Dictyogenous* and *Diegueños*. You sneaky rascal! You've stumped me!" Qwilleran had to look up both definitions, and that counted two points for the cat.

The final score was 7 to 5 in Qwilleran's favor. Then he proceeded to shower and dress, after preparing Koko's breakfast—fresh beef, diced and heated with a little canned mushroom gravy. The cat showed no interest in food, however. He followed the man around, yowling for attention in his clarion Siamese voice, tugging at the bath towel, leaping into dresser drawers as they were opened.

"What tie shall I wear?" Qwilleran asked him. There were only a few neckties in his collection— for the most part Scotch plaids with a predominance of red. They hung about the apartment on door handles and chairbacks. "Maybe I should wear something funereal to impress Percy favorably. These days we all conform. You cats are the only real independents left."

Koko blinked his acknowledgment.

Qwilleran reached for a narrow strip of navy-blue wool draped over the swing-arm of a floor lamp. "Damn those moths!" he said. "Another tie ruined!"

Koko uttered a small squeak that sounded like sympathy, and Qwilleran, examining the nibbled edge of the necktie, decided to wear it anyway.

"If you want to make yourself useful," he told

the cat, "why don't you go to work on the moths and quit wasting your time on spider webs?"

Koko had developed a curious aberration since coming to live with Qwilleran. In this dank old building spiders were plentiful, and as fast as they spun their webs, Koko devoured the glistening strands.

Qwilleran tucked the ragged end of the navy-blue tie into his shirt and pocketed his pipe, a quarter-bend bulldog. Then he tousled Koko's head in a rough farewell and left the apartment on Blenheim Place.

When he eventually arrived in the lobby of the *Daily Fluxion,* his hair was cut, his moustache was lightly trimmed, and his shoes rivaled the polish on the black marble walls. He caught a reflection of his profile in the marble and pulled in his waistline; it was beginning to show a slight convexity.

More than a few eyes turned his way. Since his arrival at the *Fluxion* seven months before—with his ample moustache, picturesque pipe, and unexplained past—Qwilleran had been a subject for conjecture. Everyone knew he had had a notable career as a crime reporter in New York and Chicago. After that, he had disappeared for a few years, and now he was holding down a quiet desk on a Midwestern newspaper, and writing, of all things, features on art!

The elevator door opened, and Qwilleran stepped aside while several members of the Women's Department filed out on their way to morning assignments or coffee breaks. As they passed, he checked them off with a calculating eye. One was too old. One was too homely. The fashion writer was too formidable. The society writer was married.

The married one looked at him with mock reproach. "You lucky dog!" she said. "Some people get all the breaks. I hate you!"

Qwilleran watched her sail across the lobby, and then he jumped on the elevator just before the automatic doors closed.

"I wonder what *that* was all about," he mumbled.

There was one other passenger on the car—a blonde clerk from the Advertising Department. "I just heard the news," she said. "Congratulations!" and she stepped off the elevator at the next floor.

A great hope was rising under Qwilleran's frayed tie as he walked into the Feature Department with its rows of green metal desks, green typewriters, and green telephones.

Arch Riker beckoned to him. "Stick around," the feature editor said. "Percy's calling a meeting at ten thirty. Probably wants to discuss that ridiculous *w* in your name. Have you seen the first edition?" He pushed a newspaper across the desk and pointed to a major headline: *Judge Qwits Bench After Graft Qwiz.*

Riker said: "No one caught the error until the papers were on the street. You've got the whole staff confused."

"It's a good Scottish name," Qwilleran said in defense. Then he leaned over Riker's desk, and said: "I've been getting some interesting vibrations this morning. I think Percy's giving me a new assignment."

"If he is, it's news to me."

"For six months I've been journalism's most ludicrous figure—a crime writer assigned to the art beat."

"You didn't have to take the job if it didn't appeal to you."

"I needed the money. *You* know that. And I was promised a desk in the City Room as soon as there was an opening."

"Lots of luck," Riker said in a minor key.

"I think something's about to break. And whatever it is, everyone knows it but you and me."

The feature editor leaned back in his chair and folded his arms. "It's axiomatic in the communications industry," he said, "that the persons most directly concerned are the last ones to know."

When the signal came from the City Room, Riker and Qwilleran filed into the managing editor's office, saying, "Morning, Harold." The boss was called Percy only behind his back.

The advertising director was there, shooting his cuffs. The photo chief was there, looking bored. The women's editor was there, wearing a brave hat of zebra fur and giving Qwilleran a prolonged friendly stare that embarrassed him. Fran Unger had a syrupy charm that he distrusted. He was wary of women executives. He had been married to one once.

Someone closed the door, and the managing editor swiveled his chair to face Qwilleran.

"Qwill, I owe you an apology," he said. "I should have discussed this with you ten days ago. You've probably been hearing rumors, and it was unfair of me to leave you in the dark. I'm sorry. I've been involved with the mayor's Civilian Committee on Crime, but that is no excuse per se."

He's really not a bad guy, Qwilleran thought, as he wriggled anxiously in his chair.

"We promised you another assignment when the right opportunity presented itself," the editor went on, "and now we have a real challenge for you! We are about to launch a project of significance to the entire newspaper industry and, I might add, a bonanza for the *Daily Fluxion* per se."

Qwilleran began to realize why everyone called the boss Percy.

The editor continued: "This city has been selected for an experiment to determine if national advertising ordinarily carried in magazines can be diverted to daily papers in major cities."

The advertising director said, "If it works, our linage will double. The revenue for the experimental year alone will be upward of a million dollars."

"The *Morning Rampage* also will be making a bid for this plum," said the editor, "but with our new presses and our color reproduction process, we can produce a superior product."

Qwilleran stroked his moustache nervously.

"It will be your job, Qwill, to produce a special Sunday supplement for fifty-two weeks—in magazine format, with plenty of color!"

Qwilleran's mind raced ahead to the possibilities. He pictured great court trials, election campaigns, political exposés, sports spectaculars, perhaps overseas coverage. He cleared his throat, and said, "This new magazine—I suppose it will be general interest?"

"General interest in its approach," said Percy, "but specific in content. We want you to publish a weekly magazine on interior design."

"On *what*?" Qwilleran said in an unintended falsetto.

"On interior decorating. The experiment is being conducted by the home-furnishings industry."

"Interior decorating!" Qwilleran felt a chill in the roots of his moustache. "I should think you'd want a woman to handle it."

Fran Unger spoke up sweetly. "The Women's Department wanted the assignment very badly, Qwill, but Harold feels a great many *men* are interested in the home today. He wants to avoid the women's slant and attract general readership to the *Gracious Abodes* magazine."

Qwilleran's throat felt as if it had swallowed his moustache. "*Gracious Abodes*? Is that the name of the thing?"

Percy nodded. "I think it conveys the right message: charm, livability, taste! You can do stories on luxury homes, high-rent apartments, residential status symbols, and the Upper Ten Percent and how they live."

Qwilleran fingered his frayed tie.

"You'll love this assignment, Qwill," the women's editor assured him. "You'll be working with decorators, and they're delightful people."

Qwilleran leaned toward the managing editor earnestly. "Harold, are you sure you want me for this beat? You know my background! I don't know the first thing about decorating."

"You did an outstanding job on the art beat without knowing the first thing about art," said Percy. "In our business, expertise can be a drawback. What this new job needs is nothing more nor less than a seasoned newsman, creative and resourceful. If you have any trouble at the start, Fran will be glad to lend a hand, I'm sure."

Qwilleran squirmed in his chair.

"Yes, of course," said the women's editor. "We can work together, Qwill, and I can steer you in the right direction." Ignoring Qwilleran's bleak reaction, she went on. "For example, you could start with the Sorbonne Studio; they do society work. Then Lyke and Starkweather; they're the largest decorating firm in town." She made a swooning gesture. "David Lyke is absolutely adorable!"

"I'll bet he is," said Qwilleran in a sullen

growl. He had his private opinion of decorators, both male and female.

"There's also Mrs. Middy, who does cozy Early American interiors. And there's a new studio called PLUG. It specializes in Planned Ugliness."

Then Percy made a remark that cast a new light on the proposal. "This assignment will carry more responsibility," he said to Qwilleran, "and naturally your classification will be adjusted. You will be advanced from senior writer to junior editor."

Qwilleran made a quick computation and came up with a figure that would finance a decent place to live and pay off some old debts. He tugged at his moustache. "I suppose I could give it a try," he said. "How soon would you want me to start?"

"Yesterday! We happen to know that the *Morning Rampage* is breaking with their supplement on October first. We'd like to beat them to the wire."

That turned the trick. The prospect of scoring a beat on the competition stirred the ink in Qwilleran's veins. His first horrified reaction to *Gracious Abodes* dissolved into a sudden sense of proprietorship. And when Fran Unger gave him a chummy smile and said, "We'll have fun with this assignment, Qwill," he felt like saying, Sister, just keep your hands off *my magazine*.

That day, during the lunch hour, Qwilleran went out and celebrated the raise in salary. He bought a can of crabmeat for Koko and a new tie for himself. Another red wool plaid.

TWO

Wearing his new tie and the better of his two suits, Qwilleran set forth with some apprehension for his first visit to a decorating studio, bracing himself for an overdose of the precious and the esoteric.

He found the firm of Lyke and Starkweather in an exclusive shopping area, surrounded by specialty shops, art galleries, and tearooms. The entrance was impressive. Huge double doors of exotically grained wood had silver door handles as big as baseball bats.

The interior displayed furniture in room settings, and Qwilleran was pleased to find one room wallpapered in a red plaid that matched his tie. Moose antlers were mounted above a fireplace made of wormeaten driftwood, and there was a sofa covered in distressed pigskin, like the hides of retired footballs.

A slender young man approached him, and the newsman asked to see Mr. Lyke or Mr. Starkweather. After a delay that seemed inauspicious, a gray-haired man appeared from behind an Oriental screen at the rear of the shop. He had a bland appearance and a bland manner.

"Mr. Lyke is the one you should talk to, if it's about publicity," he told Qwilleran, "but he's busy with a client. Why don't you just look around while you're waiting?"

"Are you Mr. Starkweather?" Qwilleran asked.

"Yes, but I think you should talk to Mr. Lyke. He's the one. . . ."

"I'd appreciate it if you'd tell me about these displays while I'm waiting." Qwilleran motioned toward the moose antlers.

"There isn't much to tell," said Starkweather with a helpless gesture.

"What's selling these days?"

"Just about everything."

"Is there any particular color that's popular?"

"No. They're all good."

"I see you have some modern stuff over there."

"We have a little of everything."

Qwilleran's interviewing technique was not

working. "What do you call that thing?" he asked, pointing to a tall secretary-desk with a bulbous base and an inlaid design of exotic birds and flowers.

"It's a desk," said Starkweather. Then his expressionless face brightened a fraction of a degree. "Here comes Mr. Lyke."

From behind the Oriental screen came a good-looking man in his early thirties. He had his arm around an elaborately hatted middle-aged woman who was smiling and blushing with pleasure.

Lyke was saying in a deep, chesty voice: "You go home, dear, and tell the Old Man you've got to have that twelve-foot sofa. It won't cost him a cent more than the last car he bought. And remember, dear, I want you to invite me to dinner the next time you're having that *superb* chocolate cake. Don't let your cook bake it. I want you to bake it yourself—for David."

While he talked, David Lyke was walking the woman rapidly toward the front door, where he stopped and kissed her temple. Then he said a beautifully timed goodbye, meaningful but not lingering.

When he turned toward Qwilleran, he recomposed his face abruptly from an expression of rapture to one of businesslike aplomb, but he could not change his eyes. He had brooding eyes with heavy lids and long lashes. Even more striking was his hair—snow white and somewhat sensational with his young suntanned face.

"I'm David Lyke," he growled pleasantly, extending a cordial hand. His eyes flickered downward for only a second, but Qwilleran felt they had appraised his plaid tie and the width of his lapel. "Come into my office, and we'll talk."

The newsman followed him into a room that had deep-gray walls. A leopard rug sprawled on the polished ebony floor. Lounge chairs, square and bulky and masculine, were covered in fabric with the texture of popcorn. On the back wall was a painting of a nude figure, her skin tones a luminous blue-gray, like steel.

Qwilleran found himself nodding in approval. "Nice office."

"Glad you like it," the decorator said. "Don't you think gray is terribly civilized? I call this shade Poppy Seed. The chairs are sort of Dried Fig. I'm sick to death of Pablum Beige and Mother's Milk White." He reached for a decanter. "How about a splash of cognac?"

Qwilleran declined. He said he would rather smoke his pipe. Then he stated his mission, and Lyke said in his rumbling voice: "I wish you hadn't called your magazine *Gracious Abodes*. It gives me visions of lavender gloves and *pêche Melba*."

"What kind of decorating do you do?" the newsman asked.

"All kinds. If people want to live like conquistadors or English barons or little French kings, we don't fight it."

"If you can find an important house for us to

photograph, we'll put it on the cover of our first issue."

"We'd like the publicity," said the decorator, "but I don't know how our clients will react. You know how it is; whenever the boys in Washington find out a taxpayer has wall-to-wall carpet in his bathroom, they audit his tax returns for the last three years." He was flipping through a card index. "I have a magnificent Georgian Colonial job, done in Champagne and Cranberry, but the lamps haven't arrived. . . . And here's an Edwardian town house in Benedictine and Plum, but there's been a delay on the draperies; the fabric manufacturer discontinued the pattern."

"Could the photographer shoot from an angle that would avoid the missing drapes?"

Lyke looked startled, but he recovered quickly and shook his head. "No, you'd have to include the windows." He browsed through the file and suddenly seized an index card. "Here's a house I'd like to see you publish! Do you know G. Verning Tait? I did his house in French Empire with built-in vitrines for his jade collection."

"Who is this Tait?" Qwilleran asked. "I'm new in this city."

"You don't know the Taits? They're one of the old families living in pseudocastles down in Muggy Swamp. You know Muggy Swamp, of course—very exclusive." The decorator made a rueful face. "Unfortunately, the clients with the longest pedigrees are the slowest to pay their bills."

"Are the Taits very social?"

"They used to be, but they live quietly now. Mrs. Tait is unwell, as they say in Muggy Swamp."

"Do you think they'd let us photograph?"

"People with Old Money always avoid publicity on their real estate," Lyke said, "but in this case I might be able to use a little persuasion."

Other possibilities were discussed, but both the decorator and newsman agreed the Tait house would be perfect: important name, spectacular décor, brilliant color, and a jade collection to add interest.

"Besides that," said Lyke with a smug smile, "it's the only job I've succeeded in getting away from the Sorbonne Studio. It would give me a lot of satisfaction to see the Tait house on the cover of *Gracious Abodes*."

"If you succeed in lining it up, call me immediately," Qwilleran said. "We're working against time on the first issue. I'll give you my home phone."

He wrote his number on a *Daily Fluxion* card and stood up to leave.

David Lyke gave him a parting handshake that was hearty and sincere. "Good luck with your magazine. And may I give you some fatherly advice?"

Qwilleran eyed the younger man anxiously.

"Never," said Lyke with an engaging smile, "*never* call draperies *drapes*."

Qwilleran returned to his office, pondering the complexities of his new beat and thinking fondly of lunch in the familiar drabness of the Press Club, where the wall color was Sirloin, Medium Rare.

On his desk there was a message to call Fran Unger. He dialed her number reluctantly.

"I've been working on our project," said the women's editor, "and I have some leads for you. Have you got a pencil ready? . . . First, there's a Greek Revival farmhouse converted into a Japanese teahouse. And then there's a penthouse apartment with carpet on the walls and ceiling, and an aquarium under the glass floor. And I know where there's an exciting master bedroom done entirely in three shades of black, except for the bed, which is brass. . . . That should be enough to fill the first issue!"

Qwilleran felt his moustache bristling. "Well, thanks, but I've got all the material I need for the first book," he said, aware that it was a rash lie.

"Really? For a beginner you're a fast worker. What have you lined up?"

"It's a long, involved story," Qwilleran said vaguely.

"I'd love to hear it. Are you going to the Press Club for lunch?"

"No," he said with hesitation. "As a matter of

fact, I'm having lunch . . . with a decorator . . . at a private club."

Fran Unger was a good newspaperwoman, and not easy to put down. "In that case, why don't we meet for drinks at the Press Club at five thirty?"

"I'm sorry," Qwilleran said in his politest voice, "but I've got an early dinner date uptown."

At five thirty he fled to the sanctuary of his apartment, carrying a chunk of liver sausage and two onion rolls for his dinner. He would have preferred the Press Club. He liked the dingy atmosphere of the club, and the size of the steaks, and the company of fellow newsmen, but for the last two weeks he had been driven to avoiding his favorite haunt. The trouble had started when he danced with Fran Unger at the Photographers' Ball. Apparently there was some magic in Qwilleran's vintage fox trot that gave her aspirations. She had been pursuing him ever since.

"I can't get rid of that woman!" he told Koko, as he sliced the liver sausage. "She's not bad-looking, but she isn't my type. I've had all the bossy females I want! Besides, I like zebra fur on zebras."

He cut some morsels of the sausage as an appetizer for Koko, but the cat was busy snapping his jaws at a thin skein of spider web that stretched between two chair legs.

Only when the telephone rang, a moment later, did Koko pay attention. Lately he had shown signs of jealousy toward the phone. Whenever

Qwilleran talked into the instrument, Koko untied his shoelaces or bit the telephone cord. Sometimes he jumped on the desk and tried to nudge the receiver away from Qwilleran's ear.

The telephone rang, and the newsman said to the mouthpiece, "Hello? . . . Yes! What's the good news?"

Immediately Koko jumped to the desk top and started making himself a pest. Qwilleran pushed him away.

"Great! How soon can we take pictures?"

Koko was pacing back and forth on the desk, looking for further mischief. Somehow he got his leg tangled in the cord, and howled in indignation.

"Sorry, I can't hear you," said Qwilleran. "The cat's raising the roof. . . . No, I'm not beating him. Hold the line."

He extricated Koko and chased him away, then wrote down the address that David Lyke gave him. "See you Monday morning in Muggy Swamp," Qwilleran said. "And thanks. This is a big help."

The telephone rang once more that evening, and the friendly voice of Fran Unger came on the wire. "Well, hello! You're home!"

"Yes," said Qwilleran. "I'm home." He was keeping an eye on Koko, who had leaped up on the desk.

"I thought you had a big date tonight."

"Got home earlier than I expected."

"I'm at the Press Club," said the sugary voice. "Why don't you come over? We're all here, drinking up a storm."

"Scram!" said Qwilleran to Koko, who was trying to dial the phone with his nose.

"What did you say?"

"I was talking to the cat." Qwilleran gave Koko a push, but the cat slanted his eyes and stood his ground, looking determined as he devised his next move.

"By the way," the wheedling voice was saying, "when are you going to invite me up to meet Koko?"

"YOW!" said Koko, aiming his deafening howl directly into Qwilleran's right ear.

"Shut up!" said Qwilleran.

"What?"

"Oh, hell!" he said, as Koko pushed an ashtray full of pipe ashes to the floor.

"Well!" Fran Unger's voice became suddenly tart. "Your hospitality overwhelms me!"

"Listen, Fran," said Qwilleran. "I've got a mess on my hands right now." He was going to explain, but there was a click in his ear. "Hello?" he said.

A dead silence was his answer, and then a dial tone. The connection had been cut. Koko was standing with one foot planted firmly on the plunger button.

THREE

When Qwilleran reported to the Photo Lab on Monday morning to pick up a man for the Muggy Swamp assignment, he found Odd Bunsen slamming gear into a camera case and voicing noisy objections. Bunsen was the *Daily Fluxion's* specialist in train wrecks and five-alarm fires, and he had just been assigned on a permanent basis to *Gracious Abodes*.

"It's an old man's job," he complained to Qwilleran. "I'm not ready to come down off the flagpoles yet."

Bunsen, who had recently climbed a skyscraper's flagpole to get a close-up of the Fourth of July fireworks, had an exuberance of qualities and defects that amused Qwilleran. He was the most daring of the photographers, had the loudest voice, and smoked the longest and most objectionable cigars. At the Press Club he was the hungriest and the thirstiest. He was raising the largest family, and his wallet was always the flattest.

"If I wasn't broke, I'd quit," he told Qwilleran as they walked to the parking lot. "For your private information, I hope this stupid magazine is a fat flop." With difficulty and mild curses he packed the camera case, tripod, lights and light stands in his small foreign two-seater.

Qwilleran, jackknifing himself into the cramped space that remained, tried to cheer up the photographer. He said, "When are you going to trade in this sardine can on a real car?"

"This is the only kind that runs on lighter fluid," said Bunsen. "I get ten miles to the squirt."

"You photographers are too cheap to buy gas."

"When you've got six kids and mortgage payments and orthodontist bills . . ."

"Why don't you cut out those expensive cigars?" Qwilleran suggested. "They must cost you at least three cents apiece."

They turned into Downriver Road, and the photographer said, "Who lined up this Muggy Swamp assignment for you? Fran Unger?"

Qwilleran's moustache bristled. "I line up my own assignments."

"The way Fran's been talking at the Press Club, I thought she was calling the plays."

Qwilleran grunted.

"She does a lot of talking after a couple of martinis," said Bunsen. "Saturday night she was hinting that you don't like girls. You must have done something that really burned her up."

"It was my cat! Fran called me at home, and Koko disconnected the phone."

"That cat's going to get you into trouble," the photographer predicted.

They merged into the expressway traffic and drove in speed and silence until they reached the Muggy Swamp exit.

Bunsen said, "Funny they never gave the place a decent name."

"You don't understand upper-class psychology," said Qwilleran. "You probably live in one of those cute subdivisions."

"I live in Happy View Woods. Four bedrooms and a big mortgage."

"That's what I mean. The G. Verning Taits wouldn't be caught dead in a place called Happy View."

The winding roads of Muggy Swamp offered glimpses of French châteaux and English manor houses, each secluded in its grove of ancient trees. The Tait house was an ornate Spanish stucco with an iron gate opening into a courtyard and a massive nail-studded door flanked by iron lanterns.

David Lyke greeted the newsmen at the door, ushering them into a foyer paved with black and white marble squares and sparkling with crystal. A bronze sphinx balanced a white marble slab on which stood a seventeen-branch candelabrum.

"Crazy!" said Bunsen.

"I suppose you want some help with your equipment," Lyke said. He signaled to a houseboy, who gave the young white-haired decorator a worshipful look with soft black eyes. "Paolo, pitch in and help these splendid people from the newspaper, and maybe they'll take your picture to send home to Mexico."

Eagerly the houseboy helped Bunsen carry in the heavy camera case and the collection of lights and tripods.

"Are we going to meet the Taits?" Qwilleran asked.

The decorator lowered his voice. "The old boy's holed up somewhere, clipping coupons and nursing his bad back. He won't come out till we yell *Jade*! He's an odd duck."

"How about his wife?"

"She seldom makes an appearance, for which we can all be thankful."

"Did you have much trouble getting their permission?"

"No, he was surprisingly agreeable," said Lyke. "Are you ready for the tour?"

He threw open double doors and led the newsmen into a living room done in brilliant green with white silk sofas and chairs. A writing desk was in ebony ornamented with gilt, and there was a French telephone on a gilded pedestal. Against the far wall stood a large wardrobe in beautifully grained wood.

"The Biedermeier wardrobe," said Lyke, raising an eyebrow, "was in the family, and we were forced to use it. The walls and carpet are Parsley Green. You can call the chairs Mushroom. The house itself is Spanish, circa 1925, and we had to square off the arches, rip up tile floors, and replaster extensively."

As the decorator moved about the room, straightening lampshades and smoothing the folds of the elaborately swagged draperies, Qwilleran stared at the splendor around him and saw dollar signs.

"If the Taits live quietly," he whispered, "why all this?"

Lyke winked. "I'm a good salesman. What he wanted was a setting that would live up to his fabulous collection of jade. It's worth three quarters of a million. That's not for publication, of course."

The most unusual feature in the living room was a series of niches in the walls, fronted with plate glass and framed with classic moldings. On their glass shelves were arranged scores of delicately carved objects in black and translucent white, artfully lighted to create an aura of mystery.

Odd Bunsen whispered, "Is that the jade? Looks like soap, if you ask me."

Qwilleran said, "I expected it to be green."

"The green jade is in the dining room," said Lyke.

The photographer started to set up his tripod and lights, and the decorator gave Qwilleran notes on the interior design.

"When you write up this place," he said, "call the Biedermeier wardrobe an *armoire,* and call the open-arm chairs *fauteuils.*"

"Wait till the guys at the *Fluxion* read this," said Qwilleran. "I'll never hear the end of it."

Meanwhile, Bunsen was working with unusual concentration, taking both color and black-and-white shots. He shifted lights and camera angles, moved furniture an inch one way or another, and spent long periods under the focusing cloth. The houseboy was a willing assistant. Paolo was almost too eager. He got in the way.

Finally Bunsen sank into a white silk chair. "I've got to park for a minute and have a smoke." He drew a long cigar from his breast pocket.

David Lyke grimaced and glanced over his shoulder. "Do you want us all to get shot? Mrs. Tait hates tobacco smoke, and she can smell it a mile away."

"Well, that squelches *that* little idea!" Bunsen said irritably, and he went back to work.

Qwilleran said to him, "We need some close-ups of the jades."

"I can't shoot through the glass."

"The glass can be removed," said Lyke. "Paolo, will you tell Mr. Tait we need the key to the cases?"

The jade collector, a man of about fifty, came at once, and his face was radiant. "Do you want to see my jades?" he said. "Which cases do you want me to open? These pictures will be in color, won't they?" His face had a scrubbed pink gleam, and he kept crimping the corners of his mouth in an abortive smile. He looked, Qwilleran thought, like a powerful man who had gone soft. His silk sports shirt exposed a heavy growth of hair on his arms, and yet there was a complete absence of hair on his head.

The plate-glass panels in the vitrines were ingeniously installed without visible hardware. Tait himself opened them, wearing gloves to prevent smudging.

Meanwhile Lyke recited a speech with affected formality: "Mr. Tait has generously agreed to share his collection with your readers, gentlemen. Mr. Tait feels that the private collector—in accumulating works of art that would otherwise appear in museums—has an obligation to the public. He is permitting these pieces to be photographed for the education and esthetic enjoyment of the community."

Qwilleran said, "May I quote you to that effect, Mr. Tait?"

The collector did not answer. He was too absorbed in his collection. Reverently he lifted a jade teapot from its place on a glass shelf. The teapot was pure white and paper-thin.

"This is my finest piece," he said, and his voice almost trembled. "The pure white is the rarest. I shouldn't show it first, should I? I should hold it back for a grand finale, but I get so excited about this teapot! It's the purest white I've ever seen, and as thin as a rose petal. You can say that in the article: thin as a rose petal."

He replaced the teapot and began to lift other items from the shelves. "Here's a Chinese bell, almost three thousand years old. . . . And here's a Mexican idol that's supposed to cure certain ailments. Not backache, unfortunately." He crimped the corners of his mouth as if enjoying a private joke that was not very funny.

"There's a lot of detail on those things," Qwilleran observed.

"Artists used to spend a whole lifetime carving a single object," Tait said. "But not all my jades are works of art." He went to the writing table and opened a drawer. "These are primitive tools made of jade. Axheads, chisels, harpoons." He laid them out on the desk top one by one.

"You don't need to take everything out," said

Qwilleran. "We'll just photograph the carved pieces," but the collector continued to empty the drawer, handling each item with awe.

"Did you ever see jade in the rough?" he said. "This is a piece of nephrite."

"Well, let's get to work," said Bunsen. "Let's start shooting this crazy loot."

Tait handed a carved medallion to Qwilleran. "Feel it."

"It's cold," said the newsman.

"It's sensuous—like flesh. When I handle jade, I feel a prickle in my blood. Do you feel a prickle?"

"Are there many books on jade?" Qwilleran asked. "I'd like to read up on it."

"Come into my library," said the collector. "I have everything that has ever been written on the subject."

He pulled volume after volume from the shelves: technical books, memoirs, adventure, fiction—all centered upon the cool, sensuous stone.

"Would you care to borrow a few of these?" he said. "You can return them at your leisure." Then he reached into a desk drawer and slipped a button-shaped object into Qwilleran's hand. "Here! Take this with you for luck."

"Oh, no! I couldn't accept anything so valuable." Qwilleran fingered the smooth rounded surface of the stone. It was green, the way he thought jade should be.

Tait insisted. "Yes, I want you to have it. Its intrinsic value is not great. Probably just a counter used in some Japanese game. Keep it as a pocket piece. It will help you write a good article about my collection." He puckered the corners of his mouth again. "And who knows? It may give you ideas. You may become a collector of jade . . . and that is the best thing that could happen to a man!"

Tait spoke the words with religious fervor, and Qwilleran, rubbing the cool green button, felt a prickle in his blood.

Bunsen photographed several groups of jade, while the collector hovered over him with nervous excitement. Then the photographer started to fold up his equipment.

"Wait!" said Lyke. "There's one more room you should see—if it's permissible. Mrs. Tait's boudoir is magnificent." He turned to his client. "What do you think?"

Qwilleran caught a significant exchange of glances between the two men.

"Mrs. Tait is unwell," the husband explained to the newsmen. "However, let me see . . . ."

He left the room and was gone several minutes. When he returned, his bald head as well as his face was unduly flushed. "Mrs. Tait is agreeable," he said, "but please take the picture as quickly as possible."

With the photographer carrying his camera on a tripod and Paolo carrying the lights, the party followed Tait down a carpeted corridor to a secluded wing of the house.

The boudoir was a combined sitting room and bedroom, lavishly decorated. Everything looked soft and downy. The bed stood under a tentlike canopy of blue silk. The chaise longue, heaped with pillows, was blue velvet. There was only one jarring note, and that was the wheelchair standing in the bay window.

Its occupant was a thin, sharp-featured woman. Her face was pinched with either pain or petulance, and her coloring was an unhealthy blond. She acknowledged the introductions curtly, all the while trying to calm a dainty Siamese cat that sat on a cushion on her lap. The cat had large lavender-blue eyes, slightly crossed.

Bunsen, with an attempt at heartiness, said, "Well, look what we've got here! A pussycat. A cross-eyed pussycat. Woof, woof!"

"Stop that!" Mrs. Tait said sharply. "You're frightening her."

In a hushed sickroom voice her husband said: "The cat's name is Yu. That's the ancient Chinese word for jade."

"Her name is not Yu," said the invalid, giving her husband a venomous look. "Her name is Freya." She stroked the animal, and the small furry body shrank into the cushion.

Bunsen turned his back to the wheelchair and started to whistle softly while adjusting the lens of his camera.

"It's taken you a long time to snap a few pictures," the woman observed. She spoke in a peculiarly throaty voice.

In defense Bunsen said, "A national magazine would take two days to photograph what I've done in one morning."

"If you're going to photograph my room," she said, "I want my cat in the picture."

A prolonged silence hung quivering in the air as everyone turned to look at the photographer.

"Sorry," he said. "Your cat wouldn't hold still long enough for a time exposure."

Coolly the woman said, "Other photographers seem to have no difficulty taking pictures of animals."

Bunsen's eyes snapped. He spoke with strained patience. "This is a long time exposure, Mrs. Tait. I've got to stop the lens down as far as possible to get the whole room in focus."

"I'm not interested in your technical problems. I want Freya in the picture!"

The photographer drew a deep breath. "I'm using a wide angle lens. The cat will be nothing but a tiny dot unless you put it right in front of the camera. And then it'll move and ruin the time exposure."

The invalid's voice became shrill. "If you can't take the picture the way I want it, don't take it at all."

Her husband went to her side. "Signe, calm yourself," he said, and with one hand waved the others out of the room.

As the newsmen drove away from Muggy Swamp, Bunsen said: "Don't forget to give me a credit line on these pictures. This job was a blinger! Do you realize I worked for three hours without a smoke? And that biddy in the wheelchair was the last straw! Besides, I don't like to photograph cats."

"That animal was unusually nervous," Qwilleran said.

"Paolo was a big help. I slipped him a couple of bucks."

"He seemed to be a nice kid."

"He's homesick. He's saving up to go back to Mexico. I'll bet Tait pays him in peanuts."

"Lyke told me the jades are worth $750,000."

"That burns me," said Bunsen. "A man like Tait can squander millions on teapots, and I have trouble paying my milk bill."

"You married guys think you've got all the problems," Qwilleran told him. "At least you've got a home! Look at me—I live in a furnished apartment, eat in restaurants, and haven't had a decent date for a month."

"There's always Fran Unger."

"Are you kidding?"

"A man your age can't be too fussy."

"Huh!" Qwilleran contracted his waistline an inch and preened his moustache. "I still consider myself a desirable prospect, but there seems to be a growing shortage of women."

"Have you found a new place to live yet?"

"I haven't had time to look."

"Why don't you put that smart cat of yours to work on it?" Bunsen suggested. "Give him the classified ads and let him make a few phone calls."

Qwilleran kept his mouth shut.

FOUR

The first issue of *Gracious Abodes* went to press too smoothly. Arch Riker said it was a bad omen. There were no ad cancellations, the copy dummied in perfectly, cutlines spaced out evenly, and the proofs were so clean it was eerie.

The magazine reached the public Saturday night, sandwiched between several pounds of Sunday paper. On the cover was an exclusive Muggy Swamp residence in bright Parsley Green and Mushroom White. The editorial pages were liberally layered with advertisements for mattresses and automatic washers. And on page two

37

was a picture of the *Gracious Abodes* editor with drooping moustache and expressionless eyes—the mug shot from his police press card.

On Sunday morning David Lyke telephoned Qwilleran at his apartment. "You did a beautiful job of writing," said the decorator in his chesty voice, "and thanks for the overstuffed credit line. But where did they get that picture of you? It makes you look like a basset hound."

For the newsman it was a gratifying day, with friends calling constantly to offer congratulations. Later it rained, but he went out and bought himself a good dinner at a seafood restaurant, and in the evening he beat the cat at the word game, 20 to 4. Koko clawed up easy catchwords like *block* and *blood, police* and *politely*.

It was almost as if the cat had a premonition; by Monday morning *Gracious Abodes* was involved with the law.

The telephone jolted Qwilleran awake at an early hour. He groped for his wristwatch on the bedside table. The hands, after he had blinked enough to see them, said six thirty. With sleep in his bones he shuffled stiffly to the desk.

"Hello?" he said dryly.

"Qwill! This is Harold!"

There was a chilling urgency in the managing editor's voice that paralyzed Qwilleran's vocal cords for a moment.

"Is this Qwilleran?" shouted the editor.

The newsman made a squeaking reply. "Speaking."

"Have you heard the news? Did they call you?" The editor's words had the sound of calamity.

"No! What's wrong?" Qwilleran was awake now.

"The police just phoned me here at home. Our cover story—the Tait house—it's been burglarized!"

"*What!* . . . What did they get?"

"Jade! A half million dollars' worth, at a rough guess. And that's not the worst. Mrs. Tait is dead. . . . Qwill! Are you there? Did you hear me?"

"I heard you," Qwilleran said in a hollow voice, as he lowered himself slowly into a chair. "I can't believe it."

"It's a tragedy per se, and our involvement makes it even worse."

"Murder?"

"No, thank God! It wasn't quite as bad as *that.* Apparently she had a heart attack."

"She was a sick woman. I suppose she heard the intruders, and—"

"The police want to talk to you and Odd Bunsen as soon as possible," said the editor. "They want to get your fingerprints."

"They want *our* fingerprints? They want to question *us?*"

"Just routine. They said it will help them sort

out the prints they find in the house. When were you there to take pictures?"

"Monday. Just a week ago." Then Qwilleran said what they were both thinking. "The publicity isn't going to do the magazine any good."

"It could ruin it! What have you got lined up for next Sunday?"

"An old stable converted into a home. It belongs to a used-car dealer who likes to see his name in the paper. I've found a lot of good houses, but the owners don't want us to use their names and addresses—for one reason or another."

"And now they've got another reason," said the editor. "And a damn good one!"

Qwilleran slowly hung up and gazed into space, weighing the bad news. There had been no interference from Koko during this particular telephone conversation. The cat was huddled under the dresser, watching the newsman intently, as if he sensed the gravity of the situation.

Qwilleran alerted Bunsen at his home in Happy View Woods, and within two hours the two newsmen were at Police Headquarters, telling their stories.

One of the detectives said, "What's your newspaper trying to do? Publish blueprints for burglary?"

The newsmen told how they had gone about photographing the interior of the house in Muggy Swamp and how Tait had produced a key and supervised the opening of the jade cases. They told how he had wanted the rarest items to be photographed.

"Who else was there when you were taking pictures?"

"Tait's decorator, David Lyke . . . and the houseboy, Paolo . . . and I caught a glimpse of a servant in the kitchen," said Qwilleran.

"Did you have any contact with the houseboy?"

"Oh, sure," said Bunsen. "He worked with me for three hours, helping with the lights and moving furniture. A good kid! I slipped him a couple of bucks."

After the brief interrogation Qwilleran asked the detectives some prying questions, which they ignored. It was not his beat, and they knew it.

On the way out of Headquarters, Bunsen said: "Glad that's over! For a while I was afraid they suspected us."

"Our profession is above suspicion," said Qwilleran. "You never hear of a newsman turning to crime. Doctors bludgeon their wives, lawyers shoot their partners, and bankers abscond with the assets. But journalists just go to the Press Club and drown their criminal inclinations."

When Qwilleran reached his office, his first move was to telephone the studio of Lyke and Starkweather. The rumbling voice of David Lyke came quickly on the line.

"Heard the news?" Qwilleran asked in tones of gloom.

"Got it on my car radio, on the way downtown," said Lyke. "It's a rough deal for you people."

"But what about Tait? He must be going out of his mind! You know how he feels about those jades!"

"You can bet they're heavily insured, and now he can have the fun of collecting all over again." The decorator's lack of sympathy surprised Qwilleran.

"Yes, but losing his wife!"

"That was inevitable. Anything could have caused her death at any moment—bad news on the stock market, a gunfight on television! And she was a miserable woman," said Lyke. "She'd been in that wheelchair for years, and all that time she made her husband and everyone else walk a tightrope. . . . No, don't waste any tears over Mrs. Tait's demise. You've got enough to worry about. How do you think it will affect *Gracious Abodes*?"

"I'm afraid people will be scared to have their homes published."

"Don't worry. I'll see that you get material," Lyke said. "The profession needs a magazine like yours. Why don't you come to my apartment for cocktails this evening? I'll have a few decorators on tap."

"Good idea! Where do you live?"

"At the Villa Verandah. That's the new apartment house that looks like a bent waffle."

Just as Qwilleran hung up, a copyboy threw a newspaper on his desk. It was the Metro edition of the *Morning Rampage*. The *Fluxion*'s competitor had played up the Tait incident on the front page, and there were pointed references to "a detailed description of the jade collection, which appeared in another newspaper on the eve of the burglary." Qwilleran smoothed his moustache vigorously with his knuckles and went to the City Room to see the managing editor, but Percy was in conference with the publisher and the business manager.

Moodily, Qwilleran sat at his desk and stared at his typewriter. He should have been working. He should have been shooting for the next deadline, but something was bothering him. It was the *timing* of the burglary.

The magazine had been distributed Saturday evening. It was some time during the following night—late Sunday or early Monday—that the burglary occurred. Within a matter of twenty-four short hours, Qwilleran figured, someone had to (*a*) read the description of the jades and (*b*) dream up the idea of stealing them and (*c*) make elaborate preparations for a rather complex maneuver. They had to devise a plan of entering the house without disturbing family or servants, work out a method of silent access to the ingeniously designed glass-covered niches, arrange for fairly careful packing of the loot, provide a means of transporting it from the house, and schedule all this so as to elude the private police. Undoubtedly Muggy Swamp had private police patrolling the community.

There had been very little time for research, Qwilleran reflected. It would require a remarkably efficient organization to carry out the operation successfully . . . unless the thieves were acquainted with the Tait house or had advance knowledge of the jade story. And if that was the case, had they deliberately timed the burglary to make *Gracious Abodes* look bad?

As Qwilleran pondered the possibilities, the first edition of the Monday *Fluxion* came off the presses, and the copyboy whizzed through the Feature Department, tossing a paper on each desk.

The Tait incident was discreetly buried on page four, and it bore an astounding headline. Qwilleran read the six short paragraphs in six gulps. The by-line was Lodge Kendall's; he was the *Fluxion*'s regular man at Police Headquarters. There was no reference to the *Gracious Abodes* story. The estimated value of the stolen jades was omitted. And there was an incredible statement from the Police Department. Qwilleran read it with a frown, then grabbed his coat and headed for the Press Club.

The Press Club occupied a soot-covered limestone fortress that had once been the county jail. The windows were narrow and barred, and mangy pigeons roosted among the blackened turrets. Inside, the old wood-paneled walls had the lingering aroma of a nineteenth-century penal institution, but the worst feature was the noise. Voices swooped across the domed ceiling, collided with other voices, and bounced back, multiplying into a deafening roar. To the newsmen this was heaven.

Today the cocktail bar on the main floor resounded with discussion and speculation on the happening in Muggy Swamp. Jewel thefts were crimes that civilized newsmen could enjoy with relish and good conscience. They appealed to the intellect, and as a rule nobody got hurt.

Qwilleran found Odd Bunsen at that end of the bar traditionally reserved for *Fluxion* staffers. He joined him and ordered a double shot of tomato juice on the rocks.

"Did you read it?" he asked the photographer.

"I read it," said Bunsen. "They're nuts."

They talked in subdued tones. At the opposite end of the mahogany bar the voices of *Morning Rampage* staffers suggested undisguised jubilation. Qwilleran glanced with annoyance at the rival crew.

"Who's that guy down there in the light suit— the one with the loud laugh?" he demanded.

"He works in their Circulation Department," Bunsen said. "He played softball against us this summer, and take my word for it—he's a creep."

"He irritates me. A woman is dead, and he's crowing about it."

"Here comes Kendall," said the photographer. "Let's see what he thinks about the police theory."

The police reporter—young, earnest, and happy in his work—was careful to exhibit a professional air of boredom.

Qwilleran beckoned him to the bar, and said, "Do you believe that stuff you wrote this morning?"

"As far as the police are concerned," said Kendall, "it's an open-and-shut case. It had nothing to do with your publication of the Tait house. It had to be an inside job. Somebody had to know his way around."

"I know," said Qwilleran. "That's what I figured. But I don't like their choice of suspect. I don't believe the houseboy did it."

"Then how do you explain his disappearance? If Paolo didn't swing with the jades and take off for Mexico, where is he?"

Bunsen said: "Paolo doesn't fit the picture. He was a nice kid—quiet and shy—very anxious to help. He's not the type."

"You photographers think you're great judges of character," Kendall said. "Well, you're wrong! According to Tait, the boy was lazy, sly, and deceitful. On several occasions Tait threatened to fire him, but Mrs. Tait always came to Paolo's defense. And because of her physical condition, her husband was afraid to cross her."

Bunsen and Qwilleran exchanged incredulous glances, and Kendall wandered away to speak to a group of TV men.

For a while Qwilleran toyed with the jade button that Tait had given him. He kept it in his pocket with his loose change. Finally he said to Bunsen, "I called David Lyke this morning."

"How's he taking it?"

"He didn't seem vitally upset. He said the jades were insured and Mrs. Tait was a miserable creature who made her husband's life one long hell."

"I'll buy that. She was a witch-and-a-half. What did he think about Paolo being mixed up in it?"

"At the time I talked to Lyke, that hadn't been announced."

Bruno, the Press Club bartender, was hovering in the vicinity, waiting for the signal.

"No more," Qwilleran told him. "I've got to eat and get back to work."

"I saw your magazine yesterday," the bartender said. "It gave me and my wife a lot of decorating ideas. We're looking forward to the next issue."

"After what happened in Muggy Swamp, you may never see a next issue," Qwilleran said. "Nobody will want to have his house published."

Bruno gave the newsman a patronizing smile. "Maybe I can help you. If you're hard up for material, you can photograph my house. We did it ourselves."

"What kind of place have you got?" Qwilleran waited warily for the answer. Bruno was known as the poor man's Leonardo da Vinci. His talents were many, but slender.

"I have what they call a monochromatic color scheme," said the bartender. "I've got Chartreuse carpet, Chartreuse walls, Chartreuse drapes, and a Chartreuse sofa."

"Very suitable for a member of your profession," said Qwilleran, "but allow me to correct you on one small detail. We *never* call draperies *drapes.*"

FIVE

Before going to the cocktail party at David Lyke's apartment, Qwilleran went home to change clothes and give the cat a slice of corned beef he had bought at the delicatessen.

Koko greeted him by flying around the room in a catly expression of joy—over chairs, under tables, around lamps, up to the top of the bookshelves, down to the floor with a thud and a grunt—making sharp turns in midair at sixty miles an hour. Lamps teetered. Ashtrays spun around. The limp curtains rippled in the breeze. Then Koko leaped on the dictionary and scratched for all he was worth—with his rear end up, his front end down, his tail pointed skyward, like a toboggan slide with a flag on top. He scratched industriously, stopped to look at Qwilleran, and scratched again.

"No time for games," Qwilleran said. "I'm going out. Cocktail party. Maybe I'll bring you home an olive."

He put on a pair of pants that had just come from the cleaner, unpinned a newly purchased shirt, and looked for his new tie. He found it draped over the arm of the sofa. There was a hole in it, center front, and Qwilleran groaned. That left only one plaid tie in good condition. He whipped it off the doorknob where it hung and tied it around his neck, grumbling to himself. Meanwhile, Koko sat on the dictionary, hopefully preparing for a game.

"No game tonight," Qwilleran told him again. "You eat your corned beef and then have a nice long nap."

The newsman set out for the party with three-fold anticipation. He hoped to make some useful contacts; he was curious about the fashionable and expensive Villa Verandah; and he was looking forward to seeing David Lyke again. He liked the man's irreverent attitude. Lyke was not what Qwilleran had expected a decorator to be. Lyke was neither precious nor a snob, and he wore his spectacular good looks with a casual grace.

The Villa Verandah, a recent addition to the

cityscape, was an eighteen-story building curved around a landscaped park, each apartment with a balcony. Qwilleran found his host's apartment alive with the sound of bright chatter, clinking glasses, and music from hidden loudspeakers.

In a pleasant rumbling voice Lyke said: "Is this your first visit to the Villa Verandah? We call this building the Architects' Revenge. The balconies are designed to be too sunny, too windy, and too dirty. The cinders that hurtle through my living room are capable of putting out an eyeball. But it's a good address. Some of the best people live in this building, several of them blind in one eye."

He opened a sliding glass door in the glass wall and showed Qwilleran the balcony, where metal furniture stood ankle-deep in water and the wind made ripples on the surface.

"The balconies become wading pools for three days after every rain," he said. "When there's a high wind, the railings vibrate and play 'Ave Maria' by the hour. And notice our unique view—a panorama of ninety-two other balconies."

The apartment itself had a warmly livable atmosphere. Everywhere there were lighted candles, books in good leather bindings, plants of the exotic type, paintings in important frames, and heaps of pillows. A small fountain in one corner was busy splashing. And the wallpaper was the most sumptuous Qwilleran had ever seen—like silver straw with a tracery of peacocks.

The predominant note was Oriental. He noticed an Oriental screen, some bowlegged black tables, and a Chinese rug in the dining room. Some large pieces of Far Eastern sculpture stood in a bed of pebbles, lighted by concealed spotlights.

Qwilleran said to Lyke, "We should photograph this."

"I was going to suggest something else in this building," said the decorator. "I did Harry Noyton's apartment—just a *pied-à-terre* that he uses for business entertaining, but it's tastefully done in wall-to-wall money. And the colors are smart—in a ghastly way. I've used Eggplant, Spinach, and Overripe Melon."

"Who is Harry Noyton?" Qwilleran asked. "The name sounds familiar."

"You must have heard of him. He's the most vocal 'silent partner' in town. Harry owns the ballpark, a couple of hotels, and *probably* the City Hall."

"I'd like to meet him."

"You will. He's dropping in tonight. I'd really like to see you publish Harry's country house in Lost Lake Hills—all artsy-craftsy contemporary—but there's an awkward situation in the family at the moment, and it might not be advisable.... Now, come and meet some of the guests. Starkweather is here—with his lovely wife, who is getting to be a middle-aged sot, but I can't say that I blame her."

Lyke's partner was sitting quietly at one end of

the sofa, but Mrs. Starkweather was circulating
diligently. There was a frantic gaiety in her aging
face, and her costume was a desperate shade of
pink. She clung to Lyke in an amorous way when
he introduced Qwilleran.

"I'm in love with David," she told the newsman, waving a cocktail glass in a wide arc. "Isn't
he just too overwhelming? Those eyes! And that
sexy voice!"

"Easy, sweetheart," said Lyke. "Do you want
your husband to shoot me?" He turned to
Qwilleran. "This is one of the hazards of the profession. We're so lovable."

After Lyke disengaged himself from Mrs. Starkweather's grip, she clung to Qwilleran's arm and
went on prattling. "Decorators give marvelous
parties! There are always lots of *men*! And the
food is always so good. David has a marvelous
caterer. But the drinks are too potent." She gig-
gled. "Do you know many decorators? They're
lots of fun. They dress so well and they dance so
well. My husband isn't really a decorator. He used
to be in the wholesale carpet business. He handles
the money at L&S. David is the one with talent. I
adore David!"

Most of the guests were decorators, Qwilleran
discovered. All the men were handsome, the ma-
jority of them young. The women were less so,
but what they lacked in beauty and youth they
made up in vivacity and impressive clothes.
Everyone had an easy charm. They complimented

Qwilleran on his new magazine, the luxuriance of his moustache, and the fragrance of his pipe tobacco.

Conversation flitted from one subject to another: travel, fashion, rare wine, ballet, and the dubious abilities of other decorators. Repeatedly, the name of Jacques Boulanger came up and was dismissed with disapproval.

No one, Qwilleran noticed, was disposed to discuss the November election or the major-league pennant race or the situation in Asia. And none of the guests seemed disturbed by the news of the Tait theft. They were merely amused that it should have happened to a client of David's.

One young man of fastidious appearance approached Qwilleran and introduced himself as Bob Orax. He had an oval aristocratic face with elevated eyebrows.

"Ordinarily," he told the newsman, "I don't follow crime news, but my family knew the Taits, and I was fascinated by the item in today's paper. I had no idea Georgie had amassed so much jade. He and Siggy haven't entertained for years! Mother went to school with Siggy in Switzerland, you know."

"No, I didn't know."

"Siggy's family had more brains than influence, Mother says. They were all scientists and architects. And it was rather a coup when Siggy married a rich American. Georgie had *hair* in those days, according to Mother."

"How did the Taits make their money?" Qwilleran asked.

"In a rather quaint and charming way. Georgie's grandfather made a mint—an absolute *mint*—manufacturing buggy whips. But Mother says Georgie himself has never had a taste for business. Monkey business, perhaps, but nothing that you can put in the bank."

"Tait was devoted to his jade collection," said Qwilleran. "I felt very bad about the theft."

"That," said Orax loftily, "is what happens when you hire cheap help. When Father was alive, he always insisted on English butlers and Irish maids. My family had money at one time. Now we get by on our connections. And I have a little shop on River Street that helps to keep the wolf from the door."

"I'd like to call on you some day," said Qwilleran. "I'm in the market for story material."

"Frankly, I doubt whether your readers are quite ready for me," said the decorator. "I specialize in Planned Ugliness, and the idea is rather advanced for the average taste. But do come! You might find it entertaining."

"By the way, who is this Jacques Boulanger I keep hearing about?"

"Boulanger?" The Orax eyebrows elevated a trifle higher. "He does work for the Duxburies, the Pennimans, and all the other old families in Muggy Swamp."

"He must be good."

"In our business," said the decorator, "success is not always an indication of excellence. . . . Bless you! You have no drink! May I get you something from the bar?"

It was not the bar that interested Qwilleran. It was the buffet. It was laden with caviar, shrimp, a rarebit in a chafing dish, marinated mushrooms, stuffed artichoke hearts, and savory meatballs in a dill sauce. As he loaded his plate for the third time, he glanced into the kitchen and saw the large stainless-steel warming oven of a professional caterer. A smiling Oriental caught his eye and nodded encouragement, and Qwilleran signaled a compliment in the man's direction.

Meanwhile a guest with a big, ungainly figure and a craggy face sauntered over to the buffet and started popping tidbits into his mouth, washing them down with gulps from a highball glass.

"I like these kids—these decorators," he said to the newsman. "They invite me to a lot of their parties. But how they ever make a living is beyond me! They live in a dream world. I'm a businessman myself—in and out of a dozen enterprises a year—and I make every investment pay off. I'm not in the racket for kicks—like these kids. *You* understand. You're a newspaperman, aren't you?"

"Jim Qwilleran from the *Daily Fluxion*."

"You newspaper guys are a good breed. You've got your feet on the ground. I know a lot of journalists. I know the managing editors of both papers, and the *Fluxion* sports editor, and your financial writer. They've all been up to my hunting lodge. Do you like hunting and fishing?"

"I haven't done much of it," Qwilleran admitted.

"To tell the truth, all we do is sit around with a bottle and shoot the breeze. You ought to come up and join us some time. . . . By the way, I'm Harry Noyton."

They shook hands, and Qwilleran said, "David tells me you have a house that might make good story material for the *Fluxion*'s new decorating magazine."

Noyton stared at his shoes for a long minute before answering. "Come in the other room where it's quiet," he said.

They went into the breakfast room and sat at a marble-topped table—the promoter with his highball glass and Qwilleran with a plate of shrimp and mushrooms.

Noyton said: "Whatever you've heard about my house in the Hills is no lie. It's terrific! And I give David all the credit—that is, Dave and my wife. She's got talent. I don't have any talent myself. All I did was go to engine college for a couple of years." He paused and gazed out the window. "But Natalie is artistic. I'm proud of her."

"I'd like to see this house."

"Well . . . here's the problem," said Noyton, taking a long drink from his glass. "The house is going to be sold. You see, Natalie and I are getting a divorce."

"Sorry to hear it," said Qwilleran. "I've been over that course myself."

"There's no trouble between us, you understand. She just wants out! She's got this crazy idea that she wants an artistic career. Can you imagine that? She's got everything in the world, but she wants to be creative, wants to starve in an attic studio, wants to make something of her life. That's what she says. And she wants it bad! Bad enough to give up the boys. I don't understand this art bug that gets into women these days."

"You have children?"

"Two sons. Two fine boys. I don't know how she can have the heart to get up and walk away from them. But those are my terms: I get complete custody of the boys, and the divorce is forever. No willy-wagging. She can't change her mind and decide to come back after a couple of months. I won't play the fool for anyone! Especially not a woman. . . . Tell me, am I right?"

Qwilleran stared at the man—aggressive, rich, lonely.

Noyton drained his drink, and said, "I'll send the boys to military school, of course."

"Is Mrs. Noyton a painter?" Qwilleran asked.

"No, nothing like that. She's got these big looms, and she wants to weave rugs and things for decorators to sell. I don't know how she's going to make a living. She won't take any money from me, and she doesn't want the house. Know anybody wants a quarter-million dollars' worth of real estate?"

"It must be quite a place."

"Say, if you want to write it up for the paper, it might help me to unload the joint. I'm leveling with you, understand."

"Is anyone living there now?"

"Caretaker, that's all. Natalie's in Reno. I'm living here at the Villa Verandah . . . Wait'll I flavor these ice cubes."

Noyton dashed to the bar, and while he was gone the Japanese caterer quietly removed Qwilleran's plate and replaced it with another, piled high.

"Like I was saying," Noyton went on, "I have this apartment that Dave decorated. That boy's got taste! Wish I had that boy's taste. I've got a wood floor imported from Denmark, a built-in bar, a fur rug—the works!"

"I wouldn't mind seeing it."

"Come on and have a look. It's right here on this floor, in the north wing."

They left the party, Noyton carrying his highball glass. "I should warn you," he said as they walked around the curving corridor, "the colors are kind of wild."

He unlocked the door to 15-F and touched a wall switch. Qwilleran gasped.

Pleasant music burst forth. Rich colors glowed

in pools of light. Everything looked soft, comfortable, but rugged.

"Do you go for this modern stuff?" Noyton asked. "Expensive as hell when it's done right."

With awe in his voice Qwilleran said: "This is great! This really gets to me."

The floor consisted of tiny squares of dark wood with a velvety oiled finish. There was a rug as shaggy as unmown grass and half as big as a squash court.

"Like the rug?" Noyton asked. "Genuine goat hair from Greece."

It was surrounded on three sides by a trio of sofas covered in natural tan suede. A chair with inviting body curves was upholstered in something incredibly soft.

"Vicuña," said Noyton. "But try that green chair. That's my favorite."

When Qwilleran relaxed in the green chair and propped his feet on the matching ottoman, an expression of beatitude spread over his face. He stroked the sculptured woolly arms. "I'd sure like to have an apartment like this," he murmured.

"And this is the bar," said Noyton with unconcealed pride as he splashed some liquor in his glass. "And the stereo is in that old Spanish chest—the only antique in the place. Cost me a fortune." He sank into the vicuña chair. "The rent for this apartment is nothing to sneeze at, either, but some good people live in this building—good people to know." He named two judges, a banker, the retired president of the university, a prominent scientist. "I know them all. I know a lot of people in this town. Your managing editor is a good friend of mine."

Qwilleran's eyes were roving over the wall of cantilevered bookshelves, the large desk topped with rust-colored leather, the sensuous rug, and the three—not one, but three—deep-cushioned sofas.

"Yes, Lyke did a great job on the decorating," he said.

"Say, you look like a regular guy," Noyton remarked with a crafty look. "How are you getting along with these decorators?"

"They seem to be a congenial bunch," said Qwilleran, ignoring the innuendo.

"That's not what I mean. Have you met Bob Orax? He's got a real problem."

"I'm used to meeting all kinds," Qwilleran said, more curtly than he had intended. He had a newsman's capacity for identifying with his beat and defending its personnel, and he resented Noyton's aspersions.

Noyton said, "That's what I admire about you news guys. Nobody throws you. You take everything in your stride."

Qwilleran swung his feet off the ottoman and hoisted himself out of the green chair. "Well, what do you say? Shall we go back where the action is?"

They returned to the party, Noyton carrying

two bottles of bourbon from his own stock, which he added to Lyke's supply.

Qwilleran complimented the decorator on the Noyton job. "Wish I could afford an apartment like his. What does a layout like that cost, anyway?"

"Too much," said the decorator. "By the way, if you ever need anything, I'll get it for you at cost, plus freight."

"What I need," said Qwilleran, "is a furnished apartment. The place where I live is being torn down to make a parking lot, and I've got to be out in ten days."

"Why don't you use Harry's apartment for a few weeks—if you like it so much?" Lyke suggested. "He's leaving for Europe, and he'll be gone a month or more."

Qwilleran blinked. "Do you think he'd be willing to sublet—at a price I could afford?"

"Let's ask him."

Noyton said, "Hell, no, I won't sublet, but if you want to use the joint while I'm gone, just move in."

"No, I'd insist on paying rent," Qwilleran said.

"Don't give me that integrity jive! I've had a lot of good treatment from the papers, and this'll give me a chance to say thanks. Besides, it's no skin off my back. Why should I take your money?"

Lyke said to Qwilleran, "There's a catch, of

course. He'll expect you to forward his mail and take telephone messages."

Qwilleran said, "There's another catch, too. I've got a cat."

"Bring him along!" said Noyton. "He can have his own room and bath. First class."

"I could guarantee that he wouldn't scratch the furniture."

"It's a deal. I'm leaving Wednesday. The keys will be at the manager's desk, including the one for the bar. Help yourself to anything. And don't be surprised if I call you twice a day from Europe. I'm a telephone bug."

Later, Lyke said to the newsman: "Thanks for getting me off the hook. Harry was expecting *me* to do his secretary service. I don't know why, but clients think they've hired a wet nurse for life when they call in a decorator."

It had happened so fast that Qwilleran could hardly believe his good fortune. Rejoicing inwardly, he made two more trips to the buffet before saying good night to his host.

As he left the apartment, he felt a tug at his sleeve. The caterer was standing at his elbow, smiling.

"You got a doggie at home?" he asked the newsman.

"No," said Qwilleran, "but—"

"Doggie hungry. You take doggie bag," said the caterer, and he pushed a foil-wrapped package into Qwilleran's hand.

SIX

"Koko, old fellow, we're moving!" Qwilleran announced happily on Tuesday morning, as he took the doggie bag from the refrigerator and prepared a breakfast for the cat and himself. Reviewing the events of the previous evening, he had to admit that the decorating beat had its advantages. Never had he received so many compliments or tasted such good food, and the offer of an apartment was a windfall.

Koko was huddling on a cushion on top of the refrigerator—the blue cushion that was his bed, his throne, his Olympus. His haunches were sticking up like fins. He looked uncomfortable, apprehensive.

"You'll like it at the Villa Verandah," Qwilleran assured him. "There are soft rugs and high bookshelves, and you can sit in the sun on the balcony. But you'll have to be on your best behavior. No flying around and busting lamps!"

Koko shifted weight. His eyes were large troubled circles of blue.

"We'll take your cushion and put it on the new refrigerator, and you'll feel right at home."

At the *Daily Fluxion* an hour later, Qwilleran reported the good news to Odd Bunsen. They met in the employees' lunchroom for their morning cup of coffee, sitting at the counter with pressmen in square paper hats, typesetters in canvas aprons, rewrite men in white shirts with the cuffs turned up, editors with their cuffs buttoned, and advertising men wearing cufflinks.

Qwilleran told the photographer, "You should see the bathrooms at the Villa Verandah! Gold faucets!"

"How do you walk into these lucky breaks?" Bunsen wanted to know.

"It was Lyke's idea, and Noyton likes to make generous gestures. He likes to be liked, and he's fascinated by newspaper people. You know the type."

"Some newspapers wouldn't let you accept a plum like that, but on a *Fluxion* salary you have to take all you can get," the photographer said. "Was there any conversation about the robbery?"

"Not much. But I picked up a little background on the Taits. Did it strike you that Mrs. Tait had a slight foreign accent?"

"She sounded as if she'd swallowed her tongue."

"I think she was Swiss. She apparently married Tait for his money, although I imagine he was a good-looking brute before he went bald."

"Did you notice his arms?" the photographer said. "Hairiest ape I ever saw! Some women go for that."

There was a tap on Bunsen's shoulder, and Lodge Kendall sat down on the next stool. "I knew I'd find you here, goldbricking as usual," he said to the photographer. "The detectives on the Tait case would like a set of the photos you took. Enlargements, preferably. Especially any shots that show the jades."

"How soon do they want them? I've got a lot of printing to do for Sunday."

"Soon as you can."

Qwilleran said, "Any progress on the case?"

"Tait has reported two pieces of luggage missing," said Kendall. "He's going away for a rest after the funeral. He's pretty shook up. And last night he went to the storeroom to get some luggage, and his two large overseas bags were gone. Paolo would need something like that to transport the jade."

"I wonder how he'd get a couple of large pieces of luggage to the airport."

"He must have had an accomplice with a car. By the time Tait found the stuff missing, Paolo had time to fly to Mexico and disappear forever in the mountains. I doubt whether they'll ever be able to trace the jades down there. Eventually they may turn up on the market, a piece at a time, but nobody will know anything about anything. You know how it is down there."

"I suppose the police have checked the airlines?"

"The passenger lists for the Sunday-night flights showed several Mexican or Spanish names. Of course, Paolo would use an alias."

Bunsen said: "Too bad I didn't take his picture. Lyke suggested it, but I never gave it another thought."

"You photographers are so stingy with your film," Kendall said, "anyone would think you had to buy it yourself."

"By the way," said Qwilleran, "exactly when did Tait discover the jades were missing?"

"About six o'clock in the morning. He's one of those early risers. He likes to go down into his workshop before breakfast and polish stones, or whatever it is he does. He went into his wife's room to see if she needed anything, found her dead, and called the doctor from the bedside phone. Then he rang for Paolo and got no response. Paolo was not in his room, and there were signs of hurried departure. Tait made a quick check of all the rooms, and that's when he discovered the display cases had been rifled."

"After which," said Qwilleran, "he called the police, and the police called Percy, and Percy called me, and it was still only six thirty. It all happened pretty fast. When Tait called the police, did he tell them about the story in *Gracious Abodes*?"

"He didn't have to. The Department had already spotted your story and questioned the advisability of describing valuable objects so explicitly."

Qwilleran snorted his disdain. "And where was the cook when all this was happening?"

"The housekeeper gets Sundays off, doesn't come back until eight o'clock Monday morning."

"And how do they account for Mrs. Tait's heart attack?"

"They assume she waked in the night, heard some kind of activity in the living room, and suspected prowlers. Evidently the fright was enough to stop her ticker, which was in bad shape, I understand."

Qwilleran objected. "That's a rambling house. The bedroom wing is half a mile from the living room. How come Mrs. Tait heard Paolo getting into the display cases—and her husband didn't?"

Kendall shrugged. "Some people are light sleepers. Chronic invalids always have insomnia."

"Didn't she try to rouse her husband? There

must be some kind of buzzer system or intercom between the two rooms."

"Look, I wasn't there!" said the police reporter. "All I know is what I hear at Headquarters." He tapped his wristwatch. "I'm due there in five minutes. See you later. . . . Bunsen, don't forget those enlargements."

When he had gone, Qwilleran said to the photographer, "I wonder where Tait's going for a rest. Mexico, by any chance?"

"You do more wondering than any three guys I know," said Bunsen, rising from the lunch counter. "I've got to do some printing. See you upstairs."

Qwilleran could not say when his suspicions first began to take a definite direction. He finished his coffee and wiped his moustache roughly with a paper napkin. Perhaps that was the moment that the gears meshed and the wheels started to turn and the newsman's deliberation began to focus on G. Verning Tait.

He went upstairs to the Feature Department and found the telephone on his desk ringing urgently. It was a green telephone, matching all the desks and typewriters in the room. Suddenly Qwilleran saw the color scheme of the office with new eyes. It was Pea Soup Green, and the walls were painted Roquefort, and the brown vinyl floor was Pumpernickel.

"Qwilleran speaking," he said into the green mouthpiece.

"Oh, Mr. Qwilleran! Is this Mr. Qwilleran himself?" It was a woman's voice, high-pitched and excited. "I didn't think they'd let me talk to you personally."

"What can I do for you?"

"You don't know me, Mr. Qwilleran, but I read every word you write, and I think your new decorating magazine is simply elegant."

"Thanks."

"Now, here's my problem. I have Avocado carpet in my dining room and Caramel *toiles de Jouy* on the walls. Should I paint the dado Caramel Custard or Avocado? And what about the lambrequins?"

When he finally got rid of his caller, Arch Riker signaled to him. "The boss is looking for you. It's urgent."

"He probably wants to know what color to paint his dado," said Qwilleran.

He found the managing editor looking thin-lipped. "Trouble!" said Percy. "That used-car dealer just phoned. You have his horsebarn scheduled for next Sunday. Right?"

"It's a remodeled stable," Qwilleran said. "Very impressive. It makes a good story. The pages are made up, and the pictures have gone to the engraver."

"He wants the story killed. I tried to persuade him to let it run, but he insists on withdrawing it."

"He was hot for it last week."

"Personally he doesn't object. He doesn't blame us for the mishap in Muggy Swamp, but his wife is worried sick. She's having hysterics. The man threatens to sue if we publish his house."

"I don't know what I can substitute in a hurry," said Qwilleran. "The only spectacular thing I have on hand is a silo painted like a barber pole and converted into a vacation home."

"Not exactly the image we want to project for *Gracious Abodes,*" said the editor. "Why don't you ask Fran Unger if she has any ideas?"

"Look, Harold!" said Qwilleran with sudden resolve. "I think we should take the offensive!"

"What do you mean?"

"I mean—conduct our own investigation! I don't buy the police theory. Pinning the crime on the houseboy is too easy. Paolo may have been an innocent dupe. For all anybody knows, he could be at the bottom of the river!"

He stopped to get the editor's reaction. Percy only stared at him.

"That was no petty theft," said Qwilleran, raising his voice, "and it was not pulled off by an unsophisticated, homesick mountain boy from an underdeveloped foreign country! Something more is involved here. I don't know who or what or why, but I've got a hunch—" He pounded his moustache with his knuckles. "Harold, why don't you assign me to cover this case? I'm sure I could dig up something of importance."

Percy waved the suggestion away impatiently.

"I'm not opposed to investigative journalism per se, but we need you on the magazine. We don't have the personnel to waste on amateur sleuthing."

"I can handle both. Just give me the credentials to talk to the police—to ask a few questions here and there."

"No, you've got enough on your hands, Qwill. Let the police handle crime. We've got to concentrate on putting out a newspaper."

Qwilleran went on as if he had not heard. He talked fast. "There's something suspicious about the timing of that incident! Someone wanted to link us with it. And that's not the only strange circumstance! Too much happened too fast yesterday morning. You called me at six thirty. What time did the police call you? And what time did they get the call from Tait? . . . And if Mrs. Tait heard sounds of prowlers, why didn't she signal her husband? Can you believe there was no intercom in that house? All that plush decorating, and not even a simple buzzer system between the invalid's bed and the sleeping quarters of her devoted husband?"

Percy looked at Qwilleran coldly. "If there's evidence of conspiracy, the police will uncover it. They know what they're doing. You keep out of it. We've got troubles enough."

Qwilleran calmed his moustache. There was no use arguing with a computer. "Do you think I should make an appearance at the funeral tomorrow?" he asked.

"It won't be necessary. We'll be adequately represented."

Qwilleran went back to his office muttering into his moustache: "Play it safe! Don't offend! Support the Advertising Department! Make money!"

"Why not?" said Arch Riker. "Did you think we were in business to disseminate news?"

At his desk Qwilleran picked up the inoffensive green telephone that was stenciled with the reminder Be Nice to People. He called the Photo Lab.

"When you make those enlargements of the jades," he said to Bunsen, "make a set of prints for me, will you? I've got an idea."

SEVEN

Qwilleran killed the cover story about the car dealer's remodeled stable and started to worry about finding a substitution. He had an appointment that morning with another decorator, but he doubted that she would be able to produce a cover story on short notice. He had talked with her on the telephone, and she had seemed flustered.

"Oh, dear!" Mrs. Middy had said. "Oh, dear! Oh, dear!"

Qwilleran went to her studio without any buoyant hope.

The sign over the door, lettered in Spencerian script, said *Interiors by Middy*. The shop was located near Happy View Woods, and it had all the ingredients of charm: window boxes filled with yellow mums, bay windows with diamond-shaped panes, a Dutch door flanked by picturesque carriage lanterns, a gleaming brass door knocker. Inside, the cozy charm was suffocating but undeniable.

As Qwilleran entered, he heard Westminster chimes, and then he saw a tall young woman emerge from behind a louvered folding screen at the back of the shop. Her straight brown hair fell like a blanket to her shoulders, hiding her forehead, eyebrows, temples and cheeks. All that was visible was a pair of roguish green eyes, an appealing little nose, an intelligent mouth, a dainty chin.

Qwilleran brightened. He said, "I have an eleven o'clock appointment with Mrs. Middy, and I don't think you're Mrs. Middy."

"I'm her assistant," said the young woman. "Mrs. Middy is a little late this morning, but then Mrs. Middy is always a little late. Would you care to sit it out?" She waved a hand dramatically around the studio. "I can offer you a Chippendale corner chair, a combback Windsor, or a mammy settle. They're all uncomfortable, but I'll talk to you and take your mind off your anguish."

"Talk to me, by all means," said Qwilleran, sitting on the mammy settle and finding that it rocked. The girl sat in the combback Windsor with her skirt well above her knees, and Qwilleran was pleased to see that they were leanly upholstered. "What's your name?" he asked, as he filled his pipe and lighted it.

"Alacoque Wright, and you must be the editor of the new Sunday supplement. I forget what you call it."

"*Gracious Abodes,*" said Qwilleran.

"Why do newspapers insist on sounding like warmed-over Horace Greeley?" Her green eyes were kidding him, and Qwilleran liked it.

"There's an element of tradition in newspapering." He glanced around the studio. "Same as in your business."

"Decorating is not really my business," said the girl crisply. "Architecture is my field, but girl architects are not largely in demand. I took this job with Mrs. Middy in desperation, and I'm afraid these imitation worm-eaten hutches and folksy-hoaxy mammy settles are warping my personality. I prefer design that reflects the spirit of our times. Down with French Empire, Portuguese Colonial and Swahili Baroque!"

"You mean you like modern design?"

"I don't like to use the word," said Miss Wright. "It's so ambiguous. There's Motel Modern, Miami Beach Modern, Borax Danish, and a lot of horrid mutations. I prefer the twentieth-century classics—the work of Saarinen, Mies van der Rohe, Breuer, and all that crowd. Mrs. Middy doesn't let me meet clients; she's afraid I'll sabotage her work. . . . And I believe I would," she added with a feline smile. "I have a sneaky nature."

"If you don't meet clients, what do you do?"

"Renderings, floor plans, color schemes. I answer the telephone and sort of sweep up. . . . But tell me about you. Do you like contemporary design?"

"I like anything," said Qwilleran, "as long as it's comfortable, and I can put my feet on it."

The girl appraised him frankly. "You're better looking than your picture in the magazine. You look serious and responsible, but also interesting. Are you married?"

"Not at the moment."

"You must feel crushed about what happened this weekend."

"You mean the theft in Muggy Swamp?"

"Do you suppose Mr. Tait will sue the *Daily Fluxion*?"

Qwilleran shook his head. "He wouldn't get to first base. We printed nothing that was untrue or libelous. And, of course, we had his permission to publish his house in the first place."

"But the robbery will damage your magazine's image, you must admit," said Miss Wright.

Just then the Dutch door opened, and a voice said, "Oh, dear! Oh, dear! Am I late?"

"Here comes Mother Middy," said the girl with the taunting eyes.

The dumpling of a woman who bustled into the studio was breathless and apologetic. She had been hurrying, and wisps of gray hair were escaping in all directions from the confinement of her shapeless mouse-gray hat.

"Get us some coffee, dear," she said to her assistant. "I'm all upset. I just got a ticket for speeding. But the officer was so kind! They have such nice policemen on the force."

The decorator sat down heavily in a black and gold rocking chair. "Why don't you write a nice article about our policemen, Mr.—Mr.—"

"Qwilleran. Jim Qwilleran," he said. "I'm afraid that's not my department, but I'd like to write a nice article about you."

"Oh, dear! Oh, dear!" said Mrs. Middy, as she removed her hat and patted her hair.

The coffee came in rosebud-covered cups, and Miss Wright served it with her eyebrows arched in disapproval of the design. Then the decorator and the newsman discussed possibilities for *Gracious Abodes*.

"I've done some lovely interiors lately," said Mrs. Middy. "Dr. Mason's house is charming, but it isn't quite finished. We're waiting for lamps. Professor Dewitt's house is lovely, too, but the draperies aren't hung."

"The manufacturers discontinued the pattern," said Qwilleran.

"Yes! How did you know?" She rocked her

chair violently. "Oh, dear! Oh, dear! What to do?"

"The housing?" her assistant whispered.

"Oh, yes, we've just finished some dormitories for the university," Mrs. Middy said, "and a sorority house for Delta Thelta, or whatever it's called. But those are out of town."

"Don't forget Mrs. Allison's," said Miss Wright.

"Oh, yes, Mrs. Allison's is really lovely. Would you be interested in a residence for career girls, Mr. Qwillum? It shows what can be done with a boardinghouse. It's one of those turn-of-the-century mansions on Merchant Street—all very gloomy and grotesque before Mrs. Allison called me in."

"It looked like a Victorian bordello," said Miss Wright.

"I used crewelwork in the living room and canopied beds in the girls' rooms. And the dining room turned out very well. Instead of one long table, which looks so institutional, I used lots of little skirted tables, like a café."

Qwilleran had been considering only private residences, but he was willing to publish anything that could be photographed in a hurry.

"What is the color scheme?" he asked.

"The theme is Cherry Red," said Mrs. Middy, "with variations. Upstairs it's all Cherry Pink. Oh, you'll love it! You'll just love it."

"Any chance of photographing this afternoon?"

"Oh, dear! That's too soon. People like to tidy up before the photographer comes."

"Tomorrow morning, then?"

"I'll call Mrs. Allison right away."

The decorator bustled to the telephone, and Alacoque Wright said to Qwilleran: "Mother Middy has done wonders with the Allison house. It doesn't look like a Victorian bordello any more. It looks like an Early American bordello."

While the arrangements were being made, Qwilleran made an arrangement of his own with Miss Wright for Wednesday evening, at six o'-clock, under the City Hall clock, and he left the Middy studio with a lilting sensation in his moustache. On the way back to the office he stopped at a gourmet shop and bought a can of smoked oysters for Koko.

That evening Qwilleran packed his books in three corrugated cartons from the grocery store and dusted his two pieces of luggage. Koko watched the process with concern. He had not touched the smoked oysters.

Qwilleran said, "What's the matter? Dieting?"

Koko began to prowl the apartment from one end to the other, occasionally stopping to sniff the cartons and utter a long, mournful howl.

"You're worried!" Qwilleran said. "You don't want to move." He picked up the cat and stroked his head reassuringly, then placed him on the open pages of the dictionary. "Come on, let's have a good rousing game to chase away the blues."

Koko dug his claws into the pages halfheartedly.

"*Balance* and *bald*," Qwilleran read. "Elementary! Two points for me. You'll have to try harder."

Koko grabbed again.

"*Kohistani* and *koolokamba*." Qwilleran knew the definition of the first, but he had to look up *koolokamba*. "A West African anthropoid ape with the head nearly bald and the face and hands black," he read. "That's great! That'll be a handy addition to my everyday vocabulary. Thanks a lot!"

At the end of nine innings Qwilleran had won, 14 to 4. For the most part Koko had turned up easy catchwords like *rook* and *root*, *frame* and *frank*.

"You're losing your knack," Qwilleran told him, and Koko responded with a long, indignant howl.

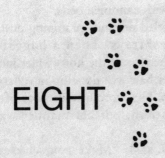

EIGHT

On Wednesday morning Qwilleran and Bunsen drove to the Allison house on Merchant Street. Qwilleran said he hoped some of the girls would be there. Bunsen said he'd like to photograph one of the canopied beds with a girl in it.

The house was a Victorian monster—the love-song of a nineteenth-century carpenter enamored of his jigsaw—but it was freshly painted, and the windows exhibited perky curtains. Mrs. Middy met them at the door, wearing her shapeless hat and a frilly lace collar.

"Where's the girls?" Bunsen shouted. "Bring on the girls!"

"Oh, they're not here in the daytime," said Mrs. Middy. "They're working girls. Now, what would you like to see? Where would you like to start?"

"What I want to see," said the photographer, "is those bedrooms with canopied beds."

The decorator bustled around, plumping cushions and moving ashtrays. Then a haggard woman came from the rear of the house. Her face was colorless, and her hair was done up in rollers, covered by a net cap. She wore a housecoat of a depressing floral pattern, but her manner was hearty.

"Hello, boys," she said. "Make yourselves at home. I've unlocked the sideboard, if you want to pour a drink."

"It's too early for hooch," said Bunsen, "even for me."

"You want some coffee?" Mrs. Allison turned her face toward the rear of the house, and shouted. *"Elsie, bring some coffee!"* To her guests she said, "Do you boys like sticky buns? . . . *Elsie, bring some sticky buns!"*

There was a piping, unintelligible reply from the kitchen.

"Then find something else!" yelled Mrs. Allison.

"It's a nice place you've got here," Qwilleran said.

"It pays to run a decent establishment," said the house mother, "and Mrs. Middy knows how to make a place comfortable. She doesn't come cheap, but she's worth every penny."

"Why did you choose Early American for your house?"

For an answer Mrs. Allison turned to the decorator. "Why did I choose Early American?"

"Because it's homey and inviting," said Mrs. Middy. "And because it is part of our national heritage."

"You can quote me," Mrs. Allison said to Qwilleran with a generous gesture. She went to the sideboard. "Sure you don't want a drink? I'm going to have one myself."

She poured a straight rye, and as the decorator showed the newsmen about the house, Mrs. Allison trailed after them, carrying her glass in one hand and the bottle in the other. Qwilleran made notes on crewelwork, dry sinks, and Queen Anne candlesticks. The photographer formed an attachment for a ship's figurehead over the living-room mantel—an old wood carving of a full-busted mermaid with chipped nose and peeling paint.

He said, "Reminds me of a girl I used to date."

"That's one I caught and had stuffed," said Mrs. Allison. "You should've seen the one that got away."

Mrs. Middy said: "Look at the skirts on these little café tables, Mr. Qwillum. Aren't they sweet?

They're slightly Victorian, but Mrs. Allison didn't want the interior to be too *pure*."

"It's all pretty elegant," Qwilleran said to the house mother. "I suppose you're fussy about the kind of girls you get in here."

"You better believe it. They gotta have references and at least two years of college." She poured another ounce in her glass.

The bedrooms were vividly pink. They had pink walls, pink carpet, and even pinker side curtains on the four-poster beds.

"Love this shade of green!" said Bunsen.

"How do the girls react to all this pink?" Qwilleran asked.

Mrs. Allison turned to the decorator. "How do the girls react to all this pink?"

"They find it warm and stimulating," said the decorator. "Notice the hand-painted mirror frames, Mr. Qwillum."

Bunsen photographed one bedroom, the living room, a corner of the dining room, and a close-up of the ship's figurehead. He was finished before noon.

"Come around and meet the girls some evening," Mrs. Allison said, as the newsmen made their goodbyes.

"Got any blondes?" asked the photographer.

"You name it. We got it."

"Okay, some night when I can get out of washing the dishes and helping the kids with their homework, I'll be around to collect that drink."

"Don't wait too long. You're not getting any younger," Mrs. Allison said cheerily.

As the newsmen carried the photographic equipment to the car, Mrs. Middy came hurrying after them. "Oh, dear! Oh, dear!" she said. "I forgot to tell you: Mrs. Allison doesn't want you to use her name or address."

"We always use names," Qwilleran said.

"Oh, dear! I was afraid so. But she thinks the girls will get crank phone calls if you print the name and address. And she wants to avoid that."

"It's newspaper policy to tell who and where," Qwilleran explained. "A story is incomplete without it."

"Oh, dear! Then we'll have to cancel the story. What a pity!"

"Cancel it! We can't cancel it! We're right on deadline!"

"Oh, dear! Then you'll have to write it up without the name and address," said Mrs. Middy.

She no longer looked like a dumpling to Qwilleran. She looked like a granite boulder in a fussy lace collar.

Bunsen said to his partner in a low voice: "You're trapped. Do what the old gal wants."

"You think I should?"

"We don't have time to pick up another cover story."

Mrs. Middy said: "Just say that it's a residence for professional girls. That sounds nicer than career girls, don't you think? And don't forget to mention the name of the decorator!" She shook a playful finger at the newsmen.

As they drove away from the house on Merchant Street, Bunsen said, "You can't win 'em all."

Qwilleran was not cheered by this philosophy, and they drove in silence until Bunsen said, "They buried the Tait woman this morning."

"I know."

"The chief assigned two photographers. That's pretty good coverage for a funeral. He only sent *one* to the international boat races last week."

Bunsen lit a cigar, and Qwilleran opened his window wide.

The photographer said, "Have you moved into the Villa Verandah with the bigwigs yet?"

"I'm moving in this afternoon. And then I've got a dinner date with Mrs. Middy's assistant."

"I hope she's got references and two years of college."

"She's quite a dish. Clever, too!"

"Look out for the clever ones," the photographer warned him. "The dumb ones are safer."

Late that afternoon Qwilleran went home, packed his two suitcases, and called a taxi. Then he proceeded to stuff the cat into a canned tuna fish carton with airholes punched in the sides. Suddenly Koko had seventeen legs, all grabbing and struggling at once, and his verbal protests added to the confusion.

"I know! I know!" shouted Qwilleran above the din. "But it's the best I can do."

When the seventeen paws, nine ears, and three tails were tucked in, and the cover clapped shut and roped, Koko found himself in a snug, dark, sheltered place, and he settled down. The only sign of life was a glistening eye, seen through one of the airholes.

Once, during the brief ride to the Villa Verandah, the taxi swerved to avoid hitting a bus, and from the back seat came an outraged scream.

"My God!" yelled the driver, slamming on the brakes. "What'd I do?"

"It's only my cat," said Qwilleran. "I've got a cat in one of these boxes."

"I thought I hit a pedestrian. What is it? A bobcat?'

"He's a Siamese. They're inclined to be outspoken."

"Oh, yeah. I've seen 'em on television. Ugly buggers."

Qwilleran's moustache curled. He was never overly generous with gratuities, but he remembered to give the driver a tip lighter than usual.

At the Villa Verandah, Koko produced earsplitting howls in the elevator, but as soon as he was released from his box in the Noyton apartment, he was speechless. For a moment he stood poised with one forepaw lifted, and the place was filled with breathless, listening cat-silence. Then his head swung from side to side as he observed the general features of the room. He walked cautiously across the sleek wood floor. He sniffed the edge of the thick-piled rug and extended one paw experimentally, but withdrew it at once. He nosed the corner of one sofa, examined the hem of the draperies, looked in the wastebasket near the desk.

Qwilleran showed Koko the new location of his sandbox and gave him his old toy mouse. "Your cushion's on the refrigerator," he told the cat. "Make yourself at home."

An unfamiliar bell rang, and Koko jumped in alarm.

"It's only the phone," Qwilleran said, picking up the receiver and seating himself importantly behind the fine leather-topped desk.

From the instrument came a voice speaking in careful English. "I have a transatlantic call for Mr. James Qwilleran."

"Speaking."

"Copenhagen calling."

Then came the excited voice of Harry Noyton. "Would you believe it? I'm in Copenhagen already! How's everything? Did you move in? Did you get settled?"

"Just got here. How was the flight?"

"Some turbulence east of Gander, but it was a good trip on the whole. Don't forward any mail till I give the signal. I'll keep in touch. And one of these days I'll have a scoop for the *Daily Fluxion*."

"A news story?"

"Something fantastic! Can't talk about it yet . . . But here's why I called: Do you like baseball? There's a pair of tickets for the charity game, stuck in my desk calendar. It's a shame to let them go to waste—especially at thirty bucks a throw."

"I'll probably have to work Saturday."

"Then give them to your pals at the paper."

"How do you like Copenhagen?"

"It looks very clean, very tidy. Lots of bicycles."

"How soon will your news break?"

"Hopefully, within a week," said Noyton. "And when it does, the *Fluxion* gets the first crack at it!"

After hanging up, Qwilleran looked for Noyton's calendar. He found it in the desk drawer—a large leather-bound book with a diary on one side and an index for telephone numbers on the other. The baseball tickets were clipped to September 26—box seats behind the dugout—and Qwilleran wondered whether he should use them or give them away. He could invite Alacoque Wright, break away from the office at noon on Saturday . . .

"Koko!" he snapped. "Get away from that book!"

The cat had risen noiselessly to the top of the desk and was sinking his claws in the edge of the telephone index. He was trying to play the game. Qwilleran's moustache twitched. He could not resist opening the book to the page Koko had selected.

On it he found the telephone numbers of a Dr.

Thomas and the well-known law firm of Teahandle, Burris, Hansblow, Maus, and Castle.

"Congratulations!" Qwilleran said to the cat. "You've cornered a Maus."

There was also Tappington, the stockbroker, and the phone number of Toledo, the most expensive restaurant in town. And at the bottom of the list there was the name Tait. Not George Tait or Verning Tait, but Signe Tait.

Qwilleran stared at the hastily scrawled name as if it were the ghost of the dead woman. Why had Noyton listed Signe and not her husband? What business did a big-time promoter have with the invalid wife of a rich, idle collector of jades?

Qwilleran recalled his conversation with Noyton at David's party. The jade theft had been discussed, but the promoter had not mentioned his acquaintance with the late Mrs. Tait. And yet he was an unabashed name-dropper, and the Tait name would have been an impressive one to drop.

Qwilleran closed the book slowly and opened it again quickly. He went through the diary, checking Noyton's appointments day by day. He started with September 20 and worked backward to January 1. There was no entry concerning Signe Tait or Muggy Swamp. But the color of ink changed around the first of September. For most of the year it had been blue. Then Noyton switched to black. Signe Tait's phone number was written in black; it had been added within the last three weeks.

NINE

Before leaving the apartment for his date with Alacoque Wright, Qwilleran telephoned David Lyke to inquire about Mrs. Tait's funeral.

"You should have been there," said the decorator. "There was enough blue blood to float a ship. All the Old Guard who knew Tait's pappy and grandpappy. You never saw so many pince-nez and Queen Mary hats."

"How was Tait taking it?"

"I wish I could say he looked pale and haggard, but with that healthy flush of his he always looks as if he'd just won at tennis. Why weren't you there?"

"I was working on a cover story. And this afternoon I moved into Harry Noyton's apartment."

"Good! We're neighbors," David said. "Why don't you come over Saturday night and meet Natalie Noyton? She just got back from Reno, and I'm having a few people in for drinks."

Qwilleran recalled the excellence of the buffet at the decorator's last party and accepted the invitation with alacrity. After that, he prepared a hasty dinner for Koko—half a can of red salmon garnished with a raw egg yolk—and said: "Be a good cat. I'll be home late and fix you a snack."

At six o'clock sharp he met Alacoque Wright under the City Hall clock; her punctuality had an architectural precision. She was wearing a curious medley of green skirt, turquoise top, and blue cape in a weave that reminded Qwilleran of dining-room chair seats somewhere in his forgotten past.

"I made it myself—out of upholstery samples," she said, peering at him from under a quantity of glossy brown hair that enveloped her head, shoulders, and much of her face.

He took her to the Press Club for dinner, aware that he was being observed by all the regulars at the bar and would have to account, the next day, for his taste in women. Nevertheless, it had to be the Press Club. He had a charge account there, and payday was not until Friday. He ushered his date—she asked Qwilleran to call her Cokey—upstairs to the main dining room, where the atmosphere was quieter and the rolls were sprinkled with poppy seeds.

"Have a cocktail?" Qwilleran invited. "I'm on the wagon myself, but I'll have a lemon and seltzer to keep you company."

Cokey looked keenly interested. "Why aren't you drinking?"

"It's a long story, and the less said about it, the better." He put a matchbook under one table leg; all the Press Club tables had a built-in wobble.

"I'm on a yoga kick myself," she said. "No liquor. No meat. But I'll make us one of nature's own cocktails if you'll order the ingredients and two champagne glasses."

When the tray arrived, she poured a little cream into each glass, filled it with ginger ale, and then produced a small wooden device from her handbag.

"I carry my own nutmeg and grate it fresh," she said, dusting the surface of the drinks with brown spice. "Nutmeg is a stimulant. The Germans put it in everything."

Qwilleran took a cautious sip. The drink had a bite. It was like Cokey—cool and smooth, with an unexpected pepperiness. "How did you decide to become an architect?" he asked.

"Maybe you haven't noticed," said Cokey, "but there are more architects named Wright than there are judges named Murphy. We seem to gravitate to the drafting board. However, the name is getting me nowhere." She stroked her long hair lovingly. "I may have to give up the struggle and find a husband."

"Shouldn't be difficult."

"I'm glad you're so confident." She set her jaw and ground some more nutmeg on her cocktail. "Tell me what you think of the decorating profession after two weeks in the velvet jungle?"

"They seem to be likable people."

"They're children! They live in a world of play." A shadow passed over Cokey's face—the sliver of face that was visible. "And, just like children, they can be cruel." She studied the grains of nutmeg clinging to the inside of her empty glass and, catlike, darted out a pink tongue to lick it clean.

A man walked past the table and said, "Hi, there, Cokey."

She looked up abruptly. "Well, hello!" she said with meaning in the inflection.

"You know him?" Qwilleran asked in surprise.

"We've met," said Cokey. "I'm getting hungry. May we order?"

She looked at the menu and asked for brook trout with a large garnish of parsley, and a small salad. Qwilleran compared her taut figure with his own well-padded beltline and felt guilty as he ordered bean soup, a hefty steak and a baked potato with sour cream.

"Are you divorced?" Cokey asked suddenly.

Qwilleran nodded.

"That's cool. Where do you live?"

"I moved into the Villa Verandah today." He waited for her eyes to open wide, and then added in a burst of honesty, "The apartment belongs to a friend who's gone abroad."

"Do you like living alone?"

"I don't live alone," said Qwilleran. "I have a cat. A Siamese."

"I adore cats," Cokey squealed. "What's your cat's name?"

Qwilleran beamed at her. People who really appreciated animals always asked their names. "His real name is Kao K'o-Kung, but he's called Koko for everyday purposes. I considered myself a dog man until I met Koko. He's a remarkable animal. Perhaps you remember the murder on Blenheim Place last spring. Koko is the cat who was involved, and if I told you some of his intellectual feats you wouldn't believe me."

"Oh, I'd believe anything about cats. They're uncanny."

"Sometimes I'm convinced Koko senses what's going to happen."

"It's true! Cats tune in with their whiskers."

"That's what I've been told," said Qwilleran, preening his moustache absently. "Koko always gives the impression that he knows more than I do, and he has clever ways of communicating. Not that he does anything uncatlike, you understand. Yet, somehow he gets his ideas across. . . . I'm not explaining this very well."

"I know exactly what you mean."

Qwilleran looked at Cokey with appreciation. These were matters he could not discuss with his friends at the *Fluxion*. With their beagles and boxers as a frame of reference, how could they understand about cats? In this one area of his life he experienced a kind of loneliness. But Cokey understood. Her mischievous green eyes had mellowed into an expression of rapport.

He reached over and took her hand—the slender, tapering hand that was playing tiddledywinks with stray poppyseeds on the tablecloth. He said, "Have you ever heard of a cat eating spider webs—or glue? Koko has started licking gummed envelopes. One day he chewed up a dollar's worth of postage stamps."

"I used to have a cat who drank soapsuds," Cokey said. "They're individualists. Does Koko scratch furniture? It was noble of your friend to let you move into his apartment with a cat."

"Koko does all his scratching on an old unabridged dictionary," Qwilleran said with a note of pride.

"How literary of him!"

"It's not really an *old* dictionary," he explained. "It's the new edition. The man Koko used to live with bought it for himself and then decided he preferred the old edition, so he gave the new one to the cat for a scratching pad."

"I admire men who admire cats."

Qwilleran lowered his voice and spoke confidentially. "We have a game we play with this dictionary. Koko exercises his claws, and I add a few words to my vocabulary . . . This is something I wouldn't want to get around the Press Club, you understand."

Cokey looked at him mistily. "I think you're wonderful," she said. "I'd love to play the game sometime."

When Qwilleran arrived home that evening, it was late, and he was exhausted. Girls like Cokey made him realize he was not so young as he used to be.

He unlocked the door of his apartment and was groping for the light switch when he saw two red sparks in the darkened living room. They glowed with a supernatural light. He had seen them before, and he knew what they were, but they always gave him a scare.

"Koko!" he said. "Is that you?"

He flipped the lights on, and the mysterious red lights in Koko's eyes were extinguished.

The cat approached with arched back, question-mark tail, and the backswept whiskers of disapproval. He made vehement one-note complaints.

"I'm sorry," said Qwilleran. "Did you think you were abandoned? You'll never believe this, but we went for a walk—a long walk. That's what lady architects like to do on a date—take you for a walk, looking at buildings. I'm bushed!" He sank into a chair and kicked off his shoes without untying the laces. "For three hours we've been looking at architecture: insensitive massing, inefficient site-planning, trite fenestration . . ."

Koko was howling impatiently at his knee, and Qwilleran picked up the cat, laid him across his shoulder, and patted the sleek fur. He could feel the muscles struggling beneath the pelt, and Koko wriggled away and jumped down.

"Is something wrong?" Qwilleran asked.

"YOW-OW!" said Koko.

He ran to the Spanish chest that housed the stereo set. It was a massive carved piece built close to the floor, resting on four bun-shaped feet. Koko plumped to the floor in front of it, stretched one foreleg, and vainly tried to reach under the chest, his brown tail tensed in a scimitar curve.

Qwilleran uttered a weary moan. He knew the cat had lost his homemade mouse—a bouquet of dried mint leaves tied in the toe of an old sock. He also knew there would be no sleeping that night until the mouse was retrieved. He looked for something to poke under the chest. Broomstick? There was no broom in the kitchen closet; the maids evidently used their own sweeping equipment. . . . Fireplace poker? There were no fireplaces at the Villa Verandah. . . . Umbrella? If Noyton owned one, he had taken it to Europe. . . . Fishing rod? Golf club? Tennis racquet? The man seemed to have no active hobbies. . . . Backscratcher? Long-handled shoehorn? Clarinet? Discarded crutch?

With Koko at his heels, yowling imperious Siamese commands, Qwilleran searched the premises. He thought wistfully of all the long, slender implements he could use: tree branch, fly swatter—buggy whip.

Eventually he lowered himself to the floor. Lying flat, he reached under the low chest and gingerly extracted a penny, a gold earring, an olive pit, a crumpled scrap of paper, several dustballs, and finally a familiar gray wad of indefinite shape.

Koko pounced on his mouse, sniffed it once without much interest, and gave it a casual whack with his paw. It went back under the Spanish chest, and Koko sauntered away to get a drink of water before retiring for the night.

But Qwilleran stayed up smoking his pipe and thinking about many things: Cokey and nutmeg cocktails, *Gracious Abodes* and Mrs. Middy's lace collar, buggy whips and the situation in Muggy Swamp. Once he went to the wastebasket and fished out the crumpled paper he had found beneath the Spanish chest. There was only a name on it: Arne Thorvaldson. He dropped it in the basket again. The gold earring he tossed in the desk drawer with the paper clips.

TEN

On the day following the funeral, Qwilleran telephoned G. Verning Tait and asked if he might call and deliver the books on jade. He said he always liked to return borrowed books promptly.

Tait acquiesced in a voice that was neither cold nor cordial, and Qwilleran could imagine the crimping of the mouth that accompanied it.

"How did you get this number?" Tait asked.

Qwilleran passed a hand swiftly over his face and hoped he was saying the right thing. "I believe this is—yes, this must be the number that David Lyke gave me."

"I was merely curious. It's an unlisted number."

Qwilleran put Noyton's address book away in the desk, stroked Koko's head for luck, and drove to Muggy Swamp in a company car. It was a wild shot, but he was hoping to see or hear something that would reinforce his hunch—his vague suspicion that all was not exactly as represented on the police record.

He had planned no particular approach—just the Qwilleran Technique. In twenty-five years of newspapering around the country he had enjoyed astounding success in interviewing criminals (described as tight-lipped), old ladies (timid), politicians (cautious), and cowboys (taciturn). He asked no prying questions on these occasions. He just smoked his pipe, murmured encouraging phrases, prodded gently, and wore an expression of sympathetic concern, which was enhanced by the sober aspect of his moustache.

Tait himself, wearing his usual high color and another kind of silk sports shirt, admitted the newsman to the glittering foyer. Qwilleran looked inquiringly toward the living room, but the double doors were closed.

The collector invited him into the library. "Did you enjoy the books?" he said. "Are you beginning to feel the lure of jade? Do you think you might like to collect?"

"I'm afraid it's beyond my means at the moment," said Qwilleran, adding a small falsehood: "I'm subletting Harry Noyton's apartment at the

Villa Verandah, and this little spree is keeping me broke."

The name brought no sign of recognition. Tait said: "You can start collecting in a modest way. I can give you the name of a dealer who likes to help beginners. Do you still have your jade button?"

"Carry it all the time!" Qwilleran jingled the contents of his trouser pocket. Then he asked solemnly, "Did Mrs. Tait share your enthusiasm for jade?"

The corners of Tait's mouth quivered. "Unfortunately, Mrs. Tait never warmed to the fascination of jade, but collecting it and working with it have been a joy and a comfort to me for more than fifteen years. Would you like to see my workshop?" He led the way to the rear of the house and down a flight of basement stairs.

"This is a rambling house," said Qwilleran. "I imagine an intercom system comes in handy."

"Please excuse the appearance of my shop," the collector said. "It is not as tidy as it should be. I've dismissed the housekeeper. I'm getting ready to go away."

"I suppose you'll be traveling to jade country," said Qwilleran hopefully.

His supposition got no verification.

Tait said: "Have you ever seen a lapidary shop? It's strange, but when I am down here in this hideaway, cutting and polishing, I forget everything. My back ailment gives me no discomfort, and I am a happy man." He handed the newsman a small carved dragon. "This is the piece the police found behind Paolo's bed when they searched his room. It's a fairly simple design. I've been trying to copy it."

"You must feel very bitter about that boy," Qwilleran said.

Tait averted his eyes. "Bitterness accomplishes nothing."

"Frankly, his implication came as a shock to me. He seemed an open, ingenuous young man."

"People are not always what they seem."

"Could it be that Paolo was used as a tool by the real organizers of the crime?"

"That is a possibility, of course, but it doesn't bring back my jades."

"Mr. Tait," said Qwilleran, "for what it is worth, I want you to know I have a strong feeling the stolen objects will be found."

"I wish I could share your optimism." Then the collector showed a spark of curiosity. "What makes you feel that way?"

"There's a rumor at the paper that the police are on the track of something." It was not the first time Qwilleran had spread the rumor of a rumor, and it often got results.

"Strange they have not communicated with me," said Tait. He led the way up the stairs and to the front door.

"Perhaps I shouldn't have mentioned it," Qwilleran said. Then casually he remarked, "That housekeeper of yours—would she take a temporary job while you're away? A friend of mine will need a housekeeper while his wife is in the hospital, and it's hard to get good help on a short-term basis."

"I have no doubt that Mrs. Hawkins needs work," said Tait.

"How long before you'll be needing her again?"

"I don't intend to take her back," said Tait. "Her work is satisfactory, but she has an unfortunate personality."

"If you don't mind, then, I'd like to give her phone number to my friend."

Tait stepped into his library and wrote the information on a slip of paper. "I'll also give you the name and address of that jade dealer in Chicago," he said, "just in case you change your mind."

As they passed the living room Qwilleran looked hungrily at the closed doors. "Did Paolo do any damage in opening the cases?"

"No. No damage. It's small comfort," Tait said sadly, "but I like to think the jades were taken by someone who loved them."

As Qwilleran drove away from Muggy Swamp, he felt that he had wasted a morning and two gallons of *Daily Fluxion* gas. Yet, throughout the visit, he had felt a teasing discomfort about the upper lip. He thought he sensed something false in the collector's pose. The man should have been

sadder—or madder. And then there was that
heart-wringing curtain line: "I like to think the
jades were stolen by someone who loved them."

"Oh, brother!" Qwilleran said aloud. "What a
ham!"

His morning of snooping had only whetted his
curiosity, and now he headed for the place where
he might get some answers to his questions. He
drove to the shop called PLUG on River Street.

It was an unlikely spot for a decorating studio.
PLUG looked self-consciously dapper among the
dilapidated storefronts devoted to plumbing supplies and used cash registers.

The merchandise in the window was attrac-
tively arranged against a background of kitchen
oilcloth in a pink kitten design. There were vases
of ostrich plumes, chunks of broken concrete
painted in phosphorescent colors, and bowls of
eggs trimmed with sequins. The price tags were
small and refined, befitting an exclusive shop: $5
each for the eggs, $15 for a chunk of concrete.

Qwilleran walked into the shop (the door handle was a gilded replica of the Statue of Liberty),
and a bell announced his presence by tinkling the
four notes of "How Dry I Am." Immediately,
from behind a folding screen composed of old
Reader's Digest covers, came the genial propri-
etor, Bob Orax, looking more fastidious than ever
among the tawdry merchandise. There were paper
flowers pressed under glass, trays decorated with
cigar bands, and candelabra made out of steer

horns, standing on crocheted doilies. One entire wall was paved with a mosaic of pop-bottle caps. Others were decorated with supermarket ads and candy-bar wrappers matted in red velvet and framed in gilt.

"So this is your racket!" said Qwilleran. "Who buys this stuff?"

"Planned Ugliness appeals to those who are bored with Beauty, tired of Taste, and fed up with Function," said Orax brightly. "People can't stand too much beauty. It's against the human grain. This new movement is a revolt of the sophisticated intellectual. The conventional middle-class customer rejects it."

"Do you design interiors around this theme?"

"Definitely! I have just done a morning room for a client, mixing Depression Overstuffed with Mail Order Modern. Very effective. I paneled one wall in corrugated metal siding from an old tool-shed, in the original rust. The color scheme is Cinnamon and Parsnip with accents of Dill Weed."

Qwilleran examined a display of rattraps made into ashtrays.

"Those are little boutique items for the impulse buyer," said Orax, and he added with an arch smile, "I hope you understand that I'm not emotionally involved with this trend. True, it requires a degree of connoisseurship, but I'm in it primarily to make a buck, if I may quote Shakespeare."

Qwilleran browsed for a while and then said:

"That was a good party at David's place Monday night. I hear he's giving another one on Saturday—for Mrs. Noyton."

"I shall not be there," said Orax with regret. "Mother is giving a dinner party, and if I am not on hand to mix good stiff drinks for the guests, Mother's friends will discover how atrocious her cooking really is! Mother was not born to the apron. . . . But you will enjoy meeting Natalie Noyton. She has all the gagging appeal of a marshmallow sundae."

Qwilleran toyed with a pink plastic flamingo that lit up. "Were the Noytons and the Taits particularly friendly?" he asked.

Orax was amused. "I doubt whether they would move in the same social circles."

"Oh," said Qwilleran with an innocent expression. "I thought I had heard that Harry Noyton knew Mrs. Tait."

"Really?" The Orax eyebrows went up higher. "An unlikely pair! If it were Georgie Tait and Natalie, that might make sense. Mother says Georgie used to be quite a womanizer." He saw Qwilleran inspecting some chromium bowls. "Those are 1959 hubcaps, now very much in demand for salads and flower arrangements."

"How long had Mrs. Tait been confined to a wheelchair?"

"Mother says it happened after the scandal, and that must have been sixteen or eighteen years ago. I was away at Princeton at the time, but I understand it was quite a brouhaha, and Siggy immediately developed her indisposition."

Qwilleran patted his alerted moustache and cleared his throat before saying, "Scandal? What scandal?"

The decorator's eyes danced. "Oh, didn't you *know*? It was a juicy affair! You should look it up in your morgue. I'm sure the *Fluxion* has an extensive file on the subject." He picked up a feather duster and whisked it over a tray of tiny objects. "These are Cracker Jack prizes, circa 1930," he said. "Genuine tin, and very collectible. My knowledgeable customers are buying them as investments."

Qwilleran rushed back to the *Daily Fluxion* and asked the clerk in the library for the file on the Tait family.

Without a word she disappeared among the gray rows of head-high filing cabinets, moving with the speed of a sleepwalker. She returned empty-handed. "It's not here."

"Did someone check it out?"

"I don't know."

"Would you mind consulting whatever records you keep and telling me who signed for it?" Qwilleran said with impatience.

The clerk ambled away and returned with a yawn. "Nobody signed for it."

"Then where is it?" he yelled. "You must have a file on an important family like the Taits!"

Another clerk stood on tiptoe and called across

a row of files, "Are you talking about G. Verning Tait? It's a big file. A man from the Police Department was in here looking at it. He wanted to take it to Headquarters, but we told him he couldn't take it out of the building."

"He must have sneaked it out," said Qwilleran. "Some of those cops are connivers. . . . Where's your boss?"

The first clerk said, "It's his day off."

"Well, you tell him to get hold of the Police Department and get that file back here. Can you remember that?"

"Remember what?"

"Never mind. I'll write him a memo."

ELEVEN

On Saturday afternoon Qwilleran took Alacoque Wright to the ball park, and listened to her views on baseball.

"Of course," she said, "the game's basic appeal is erotic. All that symbolism, you know, and those sensual movements!"

She was wearing something she had made from a bedspread. "Mrs. Middy custom-ordered it for a king-size bed," she explained, "and it was delivered in queen-size, so I converted it into a costume suit."

Her converted bedspread was green corduroy

with an irregular plush pile like rows of marching caterpillars.

"Very tasteful," Qwilleran remarked.

Cokey tossed her cascade of hair. "It wasn't intended to be tasteful. It was intended to be sexy."

After dinner at a chophouse (Cokey had a crab leg and some stewed plums; Qwilleran had the works), the newsman said: "We're invited to a party tonight, and I'm going to do something rash. I'm taking you to meet a young man who is apparently irresistible to women of all ages, sizes, and shapes."

"Don't worry," said Cokey, giving his hand a blithe squeeze. "I prefer older men."

"I'm not *that* much older."

"But you're so mature. That's important to a person like me."

They rode to the Villa Verandah in a taxi, holding hands. At the building entrance they were greeted with enthusiasm by the doorman, whom Qwilleran had foresightedly tipped that afternoon. It was not a large tip by Villa Verandah standards, but it commanded a dollar's worth of attention from a man dressed like a nineteenth-century Prussian general.

They walked into the lofty lobby—all white marble, plate glass, and stainless steel—and Cokey nodded approval. She had become suddenly quiet. As they ascended in the automatic elevator, Qwilleran gave her a quick private hug.

The door to David's apartment was opened by a white-coated Oriental, and there was a flash of recognition when he saw Qwilleran. No one ever forgot the newsman's moustache. Then the host surged forward, radiating charm, and Cokey slipped her hand though Qwilleran's arm. He felt her grip tighten when Lyke acknowledged the introduction with his rumbling voice and drooping eyelids.

The apartment was filled with guests—clients of David's chattering about their analysts, and fellow decorators discussing the Spanish exhibition at the museum and the new restaurant in Greektown.

"There's a simply marvelous seventeenth-century Isabellina *vargueno* in the show."

"The restaurant will remind you of that little place in Athens near the Acropolis. You know the one."

Qwilleran led Cokey to the buffet. "When I'm with decorators," he said, "I feel I'm in a never-never land. They never discuss anything serious or unpleasant."

"Decorators have only two worries: discontinued patterns and slow deliveries," Cokey said. "They have no real problems." There was scorn in the curl of her lips.

"Such disapproval can't be purely professional. I suspect you were jilted by a decorator once."

"Or twice." She smoothed her long straight hair self-consciously. "Try these little crabmeat things. They've got lots of pepper in them."

Although Qwilleran had dined recently and well, he had no difficulty in trying the lobster salad, the crusty brown potato balls flavored with garlic, the strips of ginger-spiced beef skewered on slivers of bamboo, and the hot buttered cornbread filled with ham. He had a feeling of well-being. He looked at Cokey with satisfaction. He liked her spirit, and the provocative face peeking out from that curtain of hair, and the coltish grace of her figure.

Then he glanced over her shoulder toward the living room, and suddenly Cokey looked plain. Natalie Noyton had arrived.

Harry Noyton's ex-wife was plump in all areas except for an incongruously small waist and tiny ankles. Her face was pretty, like a peach, and she had peach-colored hair ballooning about her head.

One of the decorators said, "How did you like the Wild West, Natalie?"

"I didn't pay any attention to it," she replied in a small shrill voice. "I just stayed in a boarding-house in Reno and worked on my rug. I made one of those shaggy Danish rugs with a needle. Does anybody want to buy a handmade rug in Cocoa and Celery Green?"

"You've put on weight, Natalie."

"Ooh, have I ever! All I did was work on my rug and eat peanut butter. I love crunchy peanut butter."

Natalie was wearing a dress that matched her hair—a sheath of loosely woven wool with golden glints. A matching stole with long crinkly fringe was draped over her shoulders.

Cokey, who was giving Natalie an oblique in-
spection, said to Qwilleran: "That fabric must be
something she loomed herself, in between peanut-
butter sandwiches. It would have been smarter
without the metallic threads."

"What would an architect call that color?" he
asked.

"I'd call it a yellow-pink of low saturation and
medium brilliance."

"A decorator would call it Cream of Carrot,"
he said, "or Sweet Potato Soufflé."

After Natalie had been welcomed and teased
and flattered and congratulated by those who
knew her, David Lyke brought her to meet Qwilleran and Cokey. He told her, "The *Daily Fluxion*
might want to photograph your house in the
Hills. What do you think?"

"Do *you* want it photographed, David?"

"It's your house, darling. You decide."

Natalie said to Qwilleran: "I'm moving out as
soon as I find a studio. And then my husband—
my ex-husband—is going to sell the house."

"I hear it's really something," said the newsman.

"It's super! Simply super! David has oodles of
talent." She looked at the decorator adoringly.

Lyke explained: "I corrected some of the architect's mistakes and changed the window detail so
we could hang draperies. Natalie wove the
draperies herself. They're a work of art."

"Well, look, honey," said Natalie, "if it will do you any good, let's put the house in the paper."

"Suppose we let Mr. Qwilleran have a look at it."

"All right," she said. "How about Monday morning? I have a hair appointment in the afternoon."

Qwilleran said, "Do you have your looms at the house?"

"Ooh, yes! I have two great big looms and a small one. I'm crazy about weaving. David, honey, show them that sports coat I did for you."

Lyke hesitated for the flicker of an eyelid. "Darling, it's at the cleaner," he said. Later he remarked to Qwilleran: "I use some of her yardage out of friendship, but her work leaves a lot to be desired. She's just an amateur with no taste and no talent, so don't emphasize the hand-weaving if you publish the house."

The evening followed the usual Lyke pattern: a splendid buffet, drinks in abundance, music for dancing played a trifle too loud, and ten conversations in progress simultaneously. It had all the elements of a good party, but Qwilleran found himself feeling troubled at David Lyke's last remark. At his first opportunity he asked Natalie to dance, and said, "I hear you're going into the weaving business on the professional level."

"Yes, I'm going to do custom work for decorators," she said in her high-pitched voice that sounded vulnerable and pathetic. "David loves my weaving. He says he'll get me a lot of commissions."

She was an ample armful, and the glittering wool dress she wore was delectably soft, except for streaks of scratchiness where the fabric was shot with gold threads.

As they danced, she went on chattering, and Qwilleran's mind wandered. If this woman was banking her career on David's endorsement, she was in for a surprise. Natalie said she was hunting for a studio, and she had a cousin who was a newspaperman, and she loved smoked oysters, and the balconies at the Villa Verandah were too windy. Qwilleran said he had just moved into an apartment there, but refrained from mentioning whose. He speculated on the chances of sneaking a few tidbits from the buffet for his cat.

"Ooh, do you have a cat?" Natalie squealed. "Does he like lobster?"

"He likes anything that's expensive. I think he reads price tags."

"Why don't you go and get him? We'll give him some lobster."

Qwilleran doubted whether Koko would like the noisy crowd, but he liked to show off his handsome pet, and he went to get him. The cat was half asleep on his refrigerator cushion, and he was the picture of relaxation, sprawled on his back in a position of utter abandon, with one foreleg flung out in space and the other curled around his ears. He looked at Qwilleran upside down with half an inch of pink tongue protruding and an insane gleam in his slanted, half-closed eyes.

"Get up," said Qwilleran, "and quit looking like an idiot. You're going to a soirée."

By the time Koko arrived at the party, sitting on Qwilleran's shoulder, he had regained his dignity. At his entrance the noise swelled to a crescendo and then stopped altogether. Koko surveyed the scene with regal condescension, like a potentate honoring his subjects with his presence. He blinked not, neither did he move a whisker. His brown points were so artistically contrasted with his light body, his fur was shaded so subtly, and his sapphire eyes had such unadorned elegance that he made David Lyke's guests look gaudily overdressed.

Then the first exclamation broke through the silence, and everyone came forward to stroke the silky fur.

"Why, it feels like ermine!"

"I'm going to throw out my mink."

Koko tolerated the attention but remained aloof until Natalie spoke to him. He stretched his neck and sniffed her extended finger.

"Ooh, can I hold him?" she asked, and to Qwilleran's surprise Koko went gladly into her arms, snuggling in her woolly stole, sniffing it with serious concentration, and purring audibly.

Cokey pulled Qwilleran away. "It makes me so mad," she said, "when I think of all the trouble I take to stay thin and get my hair straightened and improve my conversation! Then *she* comes in, babbling and looking frizzy and thirty pounds overweight, and everybody goes for her, including the cat!"

Qwilleran experienced a pang of sympathy for Cokey, mixed with something else. "I shouldn't leave Koko here too long, among all these strangers," he said. "It might upset his stomach. Let's take him back to 15-F, and you can have a look at my apartment."

"I've brought my nutmeg grater," she said. "Do you happen to have any cream and ginger ale?"

Qwilleran retrieved Koko from Natalie's stole, and led Cokey around the long curving corridor to the other wing.

When he threw open the door of his apartment, Cokey paused for one breathless moment on the threshold and then ran into the living room with her arms flung wide. "It's glorious!" she cried.

"Harry Noyton calls it Scandihoovian."

"The green chair is Danish, and so is the end-wood floor," Cokey told him, "and the dining chairs are Finnish. But the whole apartment is like a designers' Hall of Fame. Bertoia, Wegner, Aalto, Mies, Nakashima! It's too magnificent! I can't bear it!" She collapsed in the cushions of a suede sofa and put her face in her hands.

Qwilleran brought champagne glasses filled with a creamy liquid, and solemnly Cokey ground the nutmeg on the bubbling surface.

"To Cokey, my favorite girl," he said, lifting his glass. "Skinny, straight-haired, and articulate!"

"Now I feel better," she said, and she kicked off her shoes and wiggled her toes in the shaggy pile of the rug.

Qwilleran lighted his pipe and showed her the new issue of *Gracious Abodes* with the Allison living room on the cover. They discussed its challenging shades of red and pink, the buxom ship's figurehead, and the pros and cons of four-poster beds with side curtains.

Koko was sitting on the coffee table with his back turned, pointedly ignoring the conversation. The curve of his tail, with its uplifted tip, was the essence of disdain, but the angle of his ears indicated that he was secretly listening.

"Hello, Koko," said the girl. "Don't you like me?"

The cat made no move. There was not even the tremor of a whisker.

"I used to have a beautiful orange cat named Frankie," she told Qwilleran sadly. "I still carry his picture in my handbag." She extracted a wad of cards and snapshots from her wallet and sorted them on the seat of the sofa, then proudly held up a picture of a fuzzy orange blob.

"It's out of focus, and the color has faded, but it's all I have left of Frankie. He lived to be fifteen years old. His parentage was uncertain, but—"

"Koko!" shouted Qwilleran. "Get away!"

The cat had silently crept up on the sofa, and he was manipulating his long pink tongue.

Qwilleran said, "He was licking that picture."

"Oh!" said Cokey, and she snatched up a small glossy photograph of a man. She slipped it into her wallet but not before Qwilleran had caught a glimpse of it. He frowned his displeasure as she went on talking about cats and grinding nutmeg into their cocktails.

"Now, tell me all about your moustache," Cokey said. "I suppose you know it's terribly glamorous."

"I raised this crop in Britain during the war," said Qwilleran, "as camouflage."

"I like it."

It pleased him that she had not said "Which war?" as young women were inclined to do. He said: "To tell the truth, I'm afraid to shave it off. I have a strange feeling that these lip whiskers put me in touch with certain things—like subsurface truths and imminent happenings."

"How wonderful!" said Cokey. "Just like cats' whiskers."

"I don't usually confide this little fact. I wouldn't want it to get noised around."

"I can see your point."

"Lately I've been getting hunches about the theft of the Tait jades."

"Haven't they found the boy yet?"

"You mean the houseboy who allegedly stole

the stuff? That's one of my hunches. I don't think he's the thief."

Cokey's eyes widened. "Do you have any evidence?"

Qwilleran frowned. "That's the trouble; I don't have a thing but these blasted hunches. The houseboy doesn't fit the role, and there's something fishy about the timing, and I have certain reservations about G. Verning Tait. Did you ever hear anything about a scandal in the Tait family?"

Cokey shook her head.

"Of course, you were too young when it happened."

Cokey looked at her watch. "It's getting late. I should be going home."

"One more drink?" Qwilleran suggested. He went to the bar with its vast liquor supply and took the cream and ginger ale from the compact refrigerator.

Cokey began walking around the room and admiring it from every angle. "Everywhere you look there's beautiful line and composition," she said with rapture in her face. "And I love the interplay of textures—velvety, sleek, woolly, shaggy. And this rug! I worship this rug!"

She threw herself down on the tumbled pile of the luxurious rug. She lay there in ecstasy with arms flung wide, and Qwilleran combed his moustache violently. She lay there, unaware that the cat was stalking her. With his tail curled down like a fishhook and his body slung low, Koko moved through the shaggy pile of the rug like a wild thing prowling through the underbrush. Then he sprang!

Cokey shrieked and sat up. "He bit me! He bit my *head*!"

Qwilleran rushed to her side. "Did he hurt you?"

Cokey ran her fingers through her hair. "No. He didn't actually bite me. He just tried to take a little nip. But he seemed so . . . *hostile*! Qwill, why would Koko do a thing like that?"

TWELVE

Qwilleran would have slept until noon on Sunday, if it had not been for the Siamese Whisker Torture. When Koko decided it was time to get up, he hopped weightlessly and soundlessly onto the sleeping man's bed and lightly touched his whiskers to nose and chin. Qwilleran opened his eyelids abruptly and found himself gazing into two enormous eyes, as innocent as they were blue.

"Go 'way," he said, and went back to sleep.

Again the whiskers were applied, this time to more sensitive areas—the cheeks and forehead.

Qwilleran winced and clenched his teeth and

his eyes, only to feel the cat's whiskers tickling his eyelids. He jumped to a sitting position, and Koko bounded from the bed and from the room, mission accomplished.

When Qwilleran shuffled out of the bedroom, wearing his red plaid bathrobe and looking aimlessly for his pipe, he surveyed the living room with heavy-lidded eyes. On the coffee table were last night's champagne glasses, the Sunday paper, and Koko, diligently washing himself all over.

"You were a bad cat last night," Qwilleran said. "Why did you try to nip that pleasant girl who's so fond of cats? Such bad manners!"

Koko rolled over and attended to the base of his tail with rapt concentration, and Qwilleran's attention went to the rug. There, in the flattened pile, was a full-length impression of Cokey's tall, slender body, where she had sprawled for one dizzy moment. He made a move to erase the imprint by kicking up the pile with his toe, but changed his mind.

Koko, finished with his morning chore, sat up on the coffee table, blinked at the newsman, and looked angelic.

"You devil!" said Qwilleran. "I wish I could read your mind. That photograph you licked—"

The telephone rang, and he went to answer it with pleased anticipation. He remembered the congratulatory calls of the previous Sunday. Now a new issue of *Gracious Abodes* had reached the public.

"Hello-o?" he said graciously.

"Qwill, it's Harold!" The tone was urgent, and Qwilleran cringed. "Qwill, have you heard the news?"

"No, I just got out of bed—"

"Your cover story in today's paper—your residence for professional girls—haven't you heard?"

"What's happened?" Qwilleran put a hand over his eyes. He had visions of mass murder—a houseful of innocent girls murdered in their beds, their four-poster beds with pink side curtains.

"The police raided it last night! It's a disorderly house!"

"*What!*"

"They planted one of their men, got a warrant, and knocked the place off."

Qwilleran sat down unexpectedly as his knees folded. "But the decorator told me—"

"How did this happen? Where did you get the tip on this—this *house?*"

"From the decorator. From Mrs. Middy, a nice little motherly woman. She specializes in—well—residences for girls. Dormitories, that is, and sorority houses. And this was supposed to be a high-class boardinghouse for professional girls."

"Professional is the word!" said Percy. "This is going to make us look like a pack of fools. Wait till the *Morning Rampage* plays it up."

Qwilleran gulped. "I don't know what to say."

"There's nothing we can do about it now, but you'd better get hold of that Mrs. Biddy—"

"Middy."

"—whatever she calls herself—and let her know exactly how we feel about this highly embarrassing incident. . . . It's an incredible situation per se, and on the heels of the Muggy Swamp mess it's too much!"

Percy hung up, and Qwilleran's stunned mind tried to remember how it had happened. There must be an explanation. Then he grabbed the telephone and dialed a number.

"Yes?" said a sleepy voice.

"Cokey!" said Qwilleran sternly. "Have you heard the news?"

"What news? I'm not awake yet."

"Well, wake up and listen to me! Mrs. Middy has got me in a jam. Why didn't you tip me off?"

"About what?"

"About Mrs. Allison's place."

Cokey yawned. "What about Mrs. Allison's place?"

"You mean you don't *know*?"

"What are you talking about? You don't make sense."

Qwilleran found himself with a death grip on the receiver. He took a deep breath. "I've just been notified that the police raided Mrs. Allison's so-called residence for professional girls last night. . . . It's a brothel! Did you know that?"

Cokey shrieked. "Oh, Qwill, what a hoot!"

"Did you know the nature of Mrs. Allison's house?" His voice was gruff.

"No, but I think the idea's a howl!"

"Well, I don't think it's a howl, and the *Daily Fluxion* doesn't think it's a howl. It makes us look like saps. How can I get hold of Mrs. Middy?"

Cokey's voice sobered. "You want to call her? Yourself? Now? . . . Oh, don't do that!"

"Why not?"

"That poor woman! She'll drop dead from mortification."

"Didn't she know what kind of establishment she was furnishing?" Qwilleran demanded.

"I'm sure she didn't. She's a genius at doing charming interiors, but she's rather . . ."

"Rather what?"

"Muddleheaded, you know. Please don't call her," Cokey pleaded. "Let me break the news gently. You don't want to *kill* the woman, do you?"

"I feel like killing somebody!"

Cokey burst into laughter again. "And in Early American!" she shrieked. "With all those Tom Jones beds!"

Qwilleran banged the receiver down. "Now what?" he said to Koko. He paced the floor for a few minutes and then snatched the telephone and dialed another number.

"Hi!" said a childish treble.

"Let me talk to Odd Bunsen," said Qwilleran.

"Hi!" said the little voice.

"Is Odd Bunsen there?"

"Hi!"

"Who is this? Where's your father? Go and get your father!"

"Hi!"

Qwilleran snorted and was about to slam the receiver down when his partner came on the line.

"That was our youngest," Bunsen said. "He's not much for conversation. What's on your mind this morning?"

Qwilleran broke the news and listened to an assortment of croaking noises as the photographer reacted wordlessly.

The newsman said with a sarcastic edge to his voice: "I just wanted you to know that you may get your wish. You hoped the magazine would fold! And these two incidents in succession may be enough to kill it."

"Don't blame me," said Bunsen. "I just take the pictures. I don't even get a credit line."

"Two issues of *Gracious Abodes* and two mishaps! It can't be accidental. I'm beginning to smell a rat."

"You don't mean the competition!"

"Who else?"

"The *Rampage* hasn't got the guts to try any dirty work."

"I know, but they've got a guy working for them who might try to pull something. You know that loudmouth in their Circulation Department? He played on their softball team, you told me."

"You mean Mike Bulmer?" Bunsen said. "He's a creep!"

"The first time I noticed him at the Press Club, I recognized the face, but it took me a long time to place it. I finally remembered him. He was mixed up in a circulation war in Chicago a few years back—a bloody affair. And now he's working at the *Rampage*. I'll bet he suggested the raid on the Allison house to the police, and I'll bet the Vice Squad was only too happy to act. You know how it is; every time the *Fluxion* editorial writers run out of ideas, they start sniping at the Vice Squad." Qwilleran tamped his moustache, and added, "I hate to say this, but I've got a nasty feeling that Cokey may be involved."

"Who?"

"This girl I've been dating. Works for Mrs. Middy. It was Cokey who suggested publishing Mrs. Allison's house, and now I've found out that she knows Bulmer. She said hello to him at the Press Club the other night."

"No law against that," Bunsen said.

"It was the way she said it! And the look she gave him! . . . There's something else, too," Qwilleran began with evident reluctance. "After the party at David Lyke's last night, I brought Cokey back to my apartment—"

"Ho HO! This is beginning to sound interesting."

"—and Koko tried to bite her."

"What was she doing to him?"

"She wasn't doing a thing! She was on the—she was minding her own business when Koko made a pass at her head. He's never done a thing like that before. I'm beginning to think he was trying to tell me something." There was silence at the other end of the line. "Are you listening?"

"I'm listening. I'm lighting a cigar."

"You get remarkably detached when you're home in Happy View Woods on Sunday. I should think you'd be more concerned about this mess."

"What mess?" Bunsen said. "I think the Allison thing is a practical joke. It's sort of funny."

"The half-million-dollar theft wasn't funny!"

"Well," Bunsen drawled, "Bulmer wouldn't go *that* far!"

"He might! Don't forget, there's a million dollars' worth of advertising involved. He might see a chance to make himself a nice bonus."

"And victimize an innocent man just to knife the competition? . . . Naw! You've seen too many old movies."

"Maybe Tait wasn't victimized," Qwilleran said slowly. "Maybe he was in on the deal."

"Brother, you're really flying high this morning."

"Goodbye," said Qwilleran. "Sorry I bothered you. Go back to your peaceful family scene."

"Peaceful!" said Bunsen. "Did you say peaceful? I'm painting the basement, and Tommy just fell in the paint bucket, and Linda threw a rag doll down the john, and Jimmy fell off the porch and blacked his eyes. You call that peaceful?"

When Qwilleran left the telephone, he wandered aimlessly through the apartment. He glanced at the shaggy rug in the living room and angrily scuffed up the pile to erase the imprint. In the kitchen he found Koko sitting on the big ragged dictionary. The cat sat tall, with forefeet pulled in close, tail curled around tightly, head cocked. Qwilleran was in no mood for games, but Koko stared at him, waiting for an affirmative.

"All right, we'll play a few innings," Qwilleran said with a sigh. He slapped the book—the starting signal—and Koko dug into the edge with the claws of his left paw.

Qwilleran flipped the pages to the spot Koko indicated—page 1102. "*Hummock* and *hungerly*," he read. "Those are easy. Find a couple of hard ones."

The cat grabbed again.

"*Feed* and *feeling*. Two more points for me."

Koko crouched in great excitement and sank his claws.

"*May queen* and *meadow mouse*," said Qwilleran, and all at once he remembered that neither he nor Koko had eaten breakfast.

As the man chopped fresh beef for the cat and warmed it in a little canned consommé, he remembered something else: In a recent game Koko had come up with the same page twice. It had happened within the last week. Twice in one game Koko had found *sacroiliac* and *sadism*. Qwilleran felt a curious tingling sensation in his moustache.

THIRTEEN

On Monday morning, as Qwilleran and Bunsen drove to Lost Lake Hills to inspect the Noyton house, Qwilleran was unusually quiet. He had not slept well. All night he had dreamed and waked and dreamed again—about interiors decorated in Crunchy Peanut Butter and Rice Pudding, with accents of Lobster and Blackstrap Molasses. And in the morning his mind was plagued by unfinished, unfounded, unfavorable thoughts.

He greatly feared that Cokey was involved in the "practical joke" on the *Fluxion,* and he didn't want it to be that way; he needed a friend like

Cokey. He was haunted, moreover, by the possibility of Tait's complicity in the plot, although his evidence was no more concrete than a disturbance on his upper lip and a peculiar experience with the dictionary. He entertained doubts about Paolo's role in the affair; was he an innocent bystander, clever criminal, accomplice, or tool? And was Tait's love affair with his jade collection genuine or a well-rehearsed act? Had the man been as devoted to his wife as people seemed to think? Was there, by any chance, another woman in his life? Even the name of the Taits' cat was veiled in ambiguity. Was it Yu or Freya?

Then Qwilleran's thoughts turned to his own cat. Once before, when the crime was murder, Koko had flushed out more clues with his cold wet nose than the Homicide Bureau had unearthed by official investigation. Koko seemed to sense without the formality of cogitation. Instinct, it appeared, bypassed his brain and directed his claws to scratch and his nose to sniff in the right place at the right time. Or was it happenstance? Was it a coincidence that Koko turned the pages of the dictionary to *hungerly* and *feed* when breakfast was behind schedule?

Several times on Sunday afternoon Qwilleran had suggested playing the word game, hoping for additional revelations, but the catchwords that Koko turned up were insignificant: *oppositional* and *optimism, cynegetic* and *cypripedium.* Qwilleran entertained little *optimism;* and *cypri-*

pedium, which turned out to be a type of orchid also called lady's-slipper, only reminded him of Cokey's toes wiggling in the luxuriant pile of the goat-hair rug.

Still, Qwilleran's notion about Koko and the dictionary persisted. A tremor ran through Qwilleran's moustache.

Odd Bunsen, at the wheel of the car, asked: "Are you sick or something? You're sitting there shivering and not saying a word."

"It's chilly," said Qwilleran. "I should have worn a topcoat." He groped in his pocket for his pipe.

"I brought a raincoat," said Bunsen. "The way the wind's blowing from the northeast, we're going to get a storm."

The trip to Lost Lake Hills took them through the suburbs and into farm country, where the maple trees were beginning to turn yellow. From time to time the photographer gave a friendly toot of the horn and wave of his cigar to people on the side of the road. He saluted a woman cutting grass, two boys on bicycles, an old man at a rural mailbox.

"You have a wide acquaintance in this neck of the woods," Qwilleran observed.

"Me? I don't know them from Adam," said Bunsen, "but these farmers can use a little excitement. Now they'll spend the whole day figuring who they know that drives a foreign car and smokes cigars."

They turned into a country road that showed the artful hand of a landscape designer, and Qwilleran read the directions from a slip of paper. "'Follow the lakeshore, first fork to the left, turn in at the top of the hill.'"

"When did you make the arrangements for this boondoggle?" the photographer wanted to know.

"At Lyke's party Saturday night."

"I hope they were sober. I don't put any stock in cocktail promises, and this is a long way to drive on a wild-goose chase."

"Don't worry. Everything's okay. Natalie wants David to get some credit for decorating the house, and Harry Noyton is hoping our story will help him sell the place. The property's worth a quarter million."

"I hope his wife doesn't get a penny of it," Bunsen said. "Any woman who'll give up her kids, the way she did, is a tramp."

Qwilleran said: "I got another phone call from Denmark this morning. Noyton wants his mail forwarded to Aarhus. That's a university town. I wonder what he's doing there."

"He sounds like a decent guy. Wouldn't you know he'd get mixed up with a dame like that?"

"I don't think you should judge Natalie until you've met her," Qwilleran said. "She's sincere. Not overly bright, but sincere. And I have an idea people take advantage of her gullibility."

The house at the end of the winding drive was of complex shape, its pink-brick walls standing at odd angles and its huge roof timbers shooting off in all directions.

"It's a gasser!" said Bunsen. "How do you find the front door?"

"Lyke says the house is organic contemporary. It's integrated with the terrain, and the furnishings are integrated with the structure."

They rang the doorbell, and while they waited they studied the mosaic murals that flanked the entrance—swirling abstract designs composed of pebbles, colored glass, and copper nails.

"Crazy!" said Bunsen.

They waited a considerable time before ringing the bell again.

"See? What did I tell you?" the photographer said. "No one home."

"It's a big house," said Qwilleran. "Natalie probably needs roller skates to get from her weaving studio to the front door."

A moment later there was a click in the lock, and the door swung inward a few inches, opened with caution. A woman in a maid's uniform stood there, guarding the entrance inhospitably.

"We're from the *Daily Fluxion,*" Qwilleran said.

"Yes?" said the maid, standing her ground.

"Is Mrs. Noyton home?"

"She can't see anybody today." The door began to close.

"But we have an appointment."

"She can't see anybody today."

Qwilleran frowned. "We've come a long way. She told us we could see the house. Would she mind if we took a quick look around? We expect to photograph it for the paper."

"She doesn't want anybody to take pictures of the house," the maid said. "She changed her mind."

The newsmen turned to look at each other, and the door snapped shut in their faces.

As they drove back to town, Qwilleran brooded about the rude rejection. "It doesn't sound like Natalie. What do you suppose is wrong? She was very friendly and agreeable Saturday night."

"People are different when they're drinking."

"Natalie was as sober as I was. Maybe she's ill, and the maid took it on herself to brush us off."

"If you want my opinion," said Bunsen, "I think your Natalie is off her rocker."

"Stop at the first phone booth," said Qwilleran. "I want to make a call."

From a booth at a country crossroad the newsman dialed the studio of Lyke and Starkweather and talked to David. "What's going on?" he demanded. "We drove all the way to Lost Lake Hills, and Natalie refused to see us. The maid wouldn't even let us in to look at the layout."

"Natalie's a kook," David said. "I apologize for

her. I'll take you out there myself one of these days."

"Meanwhile, we're in a jam—with a Wednesday deadline and no really strong story for the cover."

"If it will help you, you can photograph my apartment," said David. "You don't have to give me a credit line. Just write about how people live at the Villa Verandah."

"All right. How about this afternoon? How about two o'clock?"

"Just give me time to buy some flowers and remove some art objects," the decorator said. "There are a few things I wouldn't want people to know I have. Just between you and me, I shouldn't even have them."

The newsmen had a leisurely lunch. When they eventually headed for the Villa Verandah, Qwilleran said, "Let's stop at the pet shop on State Street. I want to buy something."

They were battling the afternoon traffic in the downtown area. At every red light Bunsen saluted certain attractive pedestrians with the motorist's wolf whistle, touching his foot tenderly to the accelerator as they passed in front of his car. For every traffic officer he had a loud quip. They all knew the *Fluxion* photographer, and one of them halted traffic at a major intersection while the car with a press card in the windshield made an illegal left turn into State Street.

"What do you want at the pet shop?" Bunsen asked.

"A harness and a leash for Koko, so I can tie him up on the balcony."

"Just buy a harness," said the photographer. "I've got twelve feet of nylon cord you can have for a leash."

"What are you doing with twelve feet of nylon cord?"

"Last fall," Bunsen said, "when I was covering football games, I lowered my film from the press box on a rope, and a boy rushed it to the Lab. Those were the good old days! Now it's nothing but crazy decorators, ornery women, and nervous cats. I work like a dog, and I don't even get a credit line."

The newsmen spent three hours at David Lyke's apartment, photographing the silvery living room, the dining room with the Chinese rug, and the master bedroom. The bed was a low platform, a few inches high, completely covered with a tiger fur throw, and the adjoining dressing room was curtained off with strings of amber beads.

Bunsen said, "Those beads would last about five minutes at my house—with six kids playing Tarzan!"

In the living room the decorator had removed several Oriental objects, and now he was filling the gaps with bowls of flowers and large vases of glossy green leaves. He arranged them with a contemptuous flourish.

"Sorry about Natalie," he said, jabbing the stem of a chrysanthemum into a porcelain vase. "Now you know the kind of situation a decorator has to deal with all the time. One of my clients gave his wife the choice of being analyzed or having the house done over. She picked the decorating job, of course, and took out her neuroses on me. . . . *There*!" He surveyed the bouquet he had arranged, and disarranged it a little. He straightened some lampshades. He pressed a hidden switch and started the fountain bubbling and splashing in its bowl of pebbles. Then he stood back and squinted at the scene with a critical eye. "Do you know what this room needs?" he said. "It needs a Siamese cat on the sofa."

"Are you serious?" Qwilleran asked. "Want me to get Koko?"

Bunsen protested. "Oh, no! No nervous cats! Not in a wide-angle time exposure."

"Koko isn't nervous," Qwilleran told him. "He's a lot calmer than you are."

"And better looking," said David.

"And smarter," said Qwilleran.

Bunsen threw up his hands and looked grim, and within a few minutes Koko arrived to have his picture taken, his fur still striated from a fresh brushing.

Qwilleran placed the cat on the seat of the sofa, shifted him around at the direction of the photographer, folded one of the velvety brown forepaws under in an attitude of lordly ease, and arranged the silky brown tail in a photogenic curve. Throughout the proceeding Koko purred loudly.

"Will he stay like that without moving?" Bunsen asked.

"Sure. He'll stay if I say so."

Qwilleran gave Koko's fur a final smoothing and stepped back, saying, "Stay! Stay there!"

And Koko calmly stood up, jumped to the floor, and walked out of the room with vertical tail expressing his indifference.

"He's calm, all right," said Bunsen. "He's the calmest cat I ever met."

While the photographer finished taking pictures, Koko played with the dangling beads in David's dressing room and sniffed the tiger bed-throw with fraternal interest. Meanwhile David was preparing something for him to eat.

"Just some leftover chicken curry," the decorator explained to Qwilleran. "Yushi came over last night and whipped up an eight-boy *rijstafel*."

"Is he the one who cooks for your parties? He's a great chef!"

"He's an artist," David said softly.

David poured ginger ale for Qwilleran and Scotch for Bunsen.

The photographer said: "Does anyone want to eat at the Press Club tonight? My wife's giving a party for a gaggle of girls, and I've been kicked out of the house until midnight."

"I'd like to join you, but I've got a date," said David. "I'll take a raincheck, though. I'd like to see the inside of that club. I hear it's got all the amenities of a medieval bastille."

The two newsmen went to the Press Club bar, and Bunsen switched to double martinis while Qwilleran switched to tomato juice.

"Not such a bad day after all," said Qwilleran, "although it started out bad."

"It isn't over yet," the photographer reminded him.

"That David Lyke is quite a character, isn't he?"

"I don't know what to think about that *bedroom* of his!" said Bunsen, rolling his eyes.

Qwilleran frowned. "You know, he's an agreeable joe, but there's one thing that bugs me: he makes nasty cracks about his friends. You'd think they'd get wise, but no. Everyone thinks he's the greatest."

"When you've got looks and money, you can get away with murder."

During the next round of drinks Qwilleran said, "Do you remember hearing about a scandal in the Tait family fifteen or twenty years ago?"

"Fifteen years ago I was still playing marbles."

Qwilleran huffed into his moustache. "You must have been the only marble-player with five o'clock shadow." Then he signaled the bartender. "Bruno, do you recall a scandal involving the G. Verning Tait family in Muggy Swamp?"

The bartender shook his head with authority.

"No, I don't remember anything like that. If there'd been anything like that, I'd know about it. I have a memory like a giraffe."

Eventually the newsmen went to a table and ordered T-bone steaks.

"Don't eat the tail," Qwilleran said. "I'll take it home to Koko."

"Give him your own tail," said the photographer. "I'm not sharing my steak with any overfed cat. He lives better than I do."

"The leash is going to work fine. I tied him up on the balcony before I left. But I have to buckle the harness good and tight or he'll wiggle free. One fast flip and a tricky stretch—and he's out! That cat's a Houdini." There were other things Qwilleran wanted to confide about Koko's capabilities, but he knew better than to tell Bunsen.

After the steaks came apple pie à la mode, following which Qwilleran started on coffee and Bunsen started on brandy.

Qwilleran said, as he lighted his pipe, "I worry about Natalie—and why she wouldn't let us in today. That whole Noyton affair is mystifying. See what you can make out of these assorted facts: Natalie gets a divorce for reasons that are weak, to say the least, although we have only her husband's side of the story. I find an earring in the apartment that Harry Noyton is supposed to use for business entertaining. I also find out that he knows Mrs. Tait. Then she dies, and he leaves the country hurriedly. At the same time, Tait's jades are stolen, after which he also prepares to leave town. . . . What do you think?"

"I think the Yankees'll win the pennant."

"You're crocked!" Qwilleran said. "Let's go to my place for black coffee. Then maybe you'll be sober enough to drive home at midnight."

Bunsen showed no inclination to move.

"I should bring the cat in off the balcony, in case it rains," Qwilleran said. "Come on! We'll take your car, and I'll do the driving!"

"I can drive," said Bunsen. "Perfectly sober."

"Then take that salt shaker out of your breast pocket, and let's go."

Qwilleran drove, and Bunsen sang. When they reached the Villa Verandah, the photographer discovered that the elevator improved the resonance of his voice.

" 'Oh, how I hate to get up in the morrr-nin' —,' "

"Shut up! You'll scare the cat."

"He doesn't scare easy. He's a cool cat," said Bunsen. "A real cool cat."

Qwilleran unlocked the door of 15-F and touched a switch, flooding the living room with light.

"Where's that cool cat? I wanna see that cool cat."

"I'll let him in," Qwilleran said. "Why don't you sit down before you fall down? Try that green wing chair. It's the most comfortable thing you ever saw."

The photographer flopped into the green chair, and Qwilleran opened the balcony door. He stepped out into the night. In less than a second he was back.

"He's gone! Koko's gone!"

FOURTEEN

A twelve-foot nylon cord was tied to the handle of the balcony door. At the end of it was a blue leather harness buckled in the last notch, with the belt and the collar making a figure eight on the concrete floor.

"Somebody stole that cool cat," said the photographer from his position of authority in the green wing chair.

"Don't kid around," Qwilleran snapped at him. "This worries me. I'm going to call the manager."

"Wait a minute," said Bunsen, hauling himself out of the chair. "Let's have a good look outside."

The two men went to the balcony. They were met by a burst of high wind, and Bunsen had to steady himself.

Qwilleran peered at the adjoining balconies. "It's only about five feet between railings. Koko could jump across, I guess."

Bunsen had other ideas. He looked down at the landscaped court, fifteen stories below.

Qwilleran shuddered. "Cats don't fall from railed balconies," he said, without conviction.

"Maybe the wind blew him over."

"Don't be silly."

They gazed blankly around the curve of the building. The wind, whistling through the balcony railings, produced vibrating chords like organ music in a weird key.

Bunsen said, "Anybody around here hate cats?"

"I don't think so. I don't know. That is, I haven't—" Qwilleran was staring across the court, squinting through the darkness. The facade of the south wing was a checkerboard of light and shadow, with many of the apartments in darkness and others with a dull glow filtering through drawn draperies. But one apartment was partially exposed to view.

Qwilleran pointed. "Do you see what I see? Look at that window over there—the one where the curtains are open."

"That's David Lyke's place!"

"I know it is. And his TV is turned on. And look who's sitting on top of it, keeping warm."

The doors of a Chinese lacquer cabinet were open, and the TV screen could be seen, shimmering with abstract images. On top, in a neat bundle, sat Koko, his light breast distinct against the dark lacquer and his brown mask and ears silhouetted against the silvery wall.

"I'm going to phone Dave and see what this is all about," said Qwilleran.

He dialed the switchboard, asked for Lyke's apartment, and waited a long time before he was convinced no one was home.

"No answer," he told Bunsen.

"What now?"

"I don't know. Do you suppose Koko got lonesome and decided to go visiting?"

"He wanted some more of that curried chicken."

"He must have hopped from balcony to balcony—all the way around. Crazy cat! Lyke must have let him in and then gone out himself. He said he had a date."

"What are you going to do?" Bunsen said.

"Leave him there till morning, that's all."

"I can get him back."

"What? How could you get him back? He couldn't hear you with the door closed over there, and even if he could, how would he open the sliding door?"

"Want to bet I can't get him back?" The photographer leaped up on the side railing of the balcony and teetered there, clutching the corner post.

"No!" yelled Qwilleran. "Get down from there!" He was afraid to make a sudden move toward the man balancing on the narrow toprail. He approached Bunsen slowly, holding his breath.

"No sweat!" the photographer called out, as he leaped across the five-foot gap and grabbed the post of the next balcony. "Anything a cat can do, Odd Bunsen can do better!"

"Come back! You're out of your mind! . . . No, stay there! Don't try it again!"

"Odd Bunsen to the rescue!" yelled the photographer, as he ran the length of the balcony and negotiated the leap to the next one. But first he plucked a yellow mum from the neighbor's window box and clenched it in his teeth.

Qwilleran sat down and covered his face with his hands.

"Ya hoo!" Bunsen crowed. "Ya hoo!"

His war cries grew fainter, drowned by the whistling wind as he progressed from railing to railing around the inside curve of the Villa Verandah. Here and there a resident opened a door and looked out, without seeing the acrobatic feat being performed in the darkness.

"Ya hoo!" came a distant cry.

Qwilleran thought of the three double martinis and the two—no, three—brandies that Bunsen had consumed. He thought of the photographer's wife and six children, and his blood chilled.

There was a triumphant shout across the court, and Bunsen was waving from Lyke's balcony. He tried the sliding door; it opened. He signaled his success and then stepped into the silvery-gray living room. At his entrance Koko jumped down from his perch and scampered away.

I hope, Qwilleran told himself, that nincompoop has sense enough to bring Koko back by land and not by air.

From where the newsman stood, he could no longer see Bunsen or the cat, so he went indoors and waited for the errant pair to return. While waiting, he made two cups of instant coffee and put some cheese and crackers on a plate.

The wait was much too long, he soon decided. He went to the corridor and listened and looked down its carpeted curve. There was no sign of life—only mechanical noises from the elevator shaft and the frantic sounds of a distant TV. He returned to the balcony and scanned the south wing. There was no activity to be seen in Lyke's apartment, except for the busy images on the TV screen.

Qwilleran gulped a cup of coffee and paced the floor. Finally he went to the telephone and asked the operator to try Lyke's apartment again. The line was busy.

"What's that drunken fool doing?"

"Pardon?" said the operator.

Returning once more to the balcony, Qwilleran

stared across the court in exasperation. When his telephone rang, he jumped and sprinted for it.

"Qwill," said Bunsen's voice, several tones lower than it had been all evening. "We've got trouble over here."

"Koko? What's happened?"

"The cat's okay, but your decorator friend has *had* it."

"What do you mean?"

"Looks as if Lyke's dead."

"No! . . . No!"

"He's cold, and he's white, and there's an ugly spot on the rug. I've called the police, and I've called the paper. Would you go down to the car and get my camera?"

"I gave you the car keys."

"I put them in my raincoat pocket, and I dropped my raincoat in your front hall. I think I'd better stay here with the body."

"You sound sober all of a sudden," Qwilleran said.

"I sobered up in a hurry when I saw this."

By the time Qwilleran arrived at Lyke's apartment with Bunsen's camera, the officers from the police cruiser were there. Qwilleran scanned the living room. It was just as they had photographed it in the afternoon, except that the TV in the Chinese cabinet was yakking senselessly and there was a yellow mum on the carpet, where Bunsen had dropped it.

"As soon as I came through the door," Bunsen

said to Qwilleran, "Koko led me into the bedroom."

The body was on the bedroom floor, wrapped in a gray silk dressing gown. One finger wore a large star sapphire that Qwilleran had not seen before. The face was no longer handsome. It had lost the wit and animation that made it attractive. All that was left was a supercilious mask.

Qwilleran glanced about the room. The tiger skin had been removed from the bed, neatly folded, and laid on a bench. Everything else was in perfect order. The bed showed no indication of having been occupied.

Bunsen was hopping around the room looking for camera angles. "I just want to get one picture," he told the officers. "I won't disturb anything." To Qwilleran he said, "It's hard to get an interesting shot. The Picture Desk won't run gory stuff any more. They get complaints from the P.T.A., little old ladies, the American Legion, the D.A.R., vegetarians—"

"What did you do with Koko?" Qwilleran said.

"He's around here somewhere. Probably destroying the evidence."

Qwilleran found Koko in the dining room, sitting under the table as if nothing had happened. He had assumed his noncommittal pose, gathered in a comfortable bundle on the gold-and-blue Chinese rug, looking neither curious nor concerned nor guilty nor grieved.

When the detectives from the Homicide Bureau

arrived, Qwilleran recognized a pair he had met before. He liked the heavy-set one called Hames, a smart detective with an off-duty personality, but he didn't care for Wojcik, whose nasal voice was well suited to sarcasm.

Wojcik gave one look at Qwilleran and said, "How'd the press get here so fast?"

The patrolman said: "The photographer was here when we arrived. He let us into the apartment. He's the one who found the body and reported it."

Wojcik turned to Bunsen. "How did you happen to be here?"

"I came in through the window."

"I see. This is the fifteenth floor. And you came in through the window."

"Sure, there are balconies out there."

Hames was ogling the sumptuous living room. "Look at this wallpaper," he said. "If my wife ever saw this—"

Wojcik went into the bedroom and after that onto the balcony. He looked at the ground fifteen stories below, and he gauged the distance between balconies. Then he cornered Bunsen. "Okay, how did you get in?"

"I told you—"

"I suppose you know you smell like a distillery."

Qwilleran said: "Bunsen's telling the truth. He jumped from balcony to balcony, all the way from my place on the other side."

"This may be a silly question," said the detective, "but do you mind if I inquire *why*?"

"Well, it's like this," said the photographer. "We were across the court—"

"He came to get my cat," Qwilleran interrupted. "My cat was over here."

Hames said: "That must be the famous Siamese that's bucking for my job on the force. I'd like to meet him."

"He's in the dining room under the table."

"My wife's crazy about Siamese. Some day I've got to break down and buy her one."

Qwilleran followed the amiable detective into the dining room and said quietly: "There's something I ought to tell you, Hames. We were here this afternoon to photograph the apartment for *Gracious Abodes,* and David Lyke removed some valuable art objects before we took the pictures. I don't know what he did with them, but they were valuable, and I don't see them anywhere."

There was no reaction from the detective, who was now down on his knees under the table.

"As I recall," Qwilleran went on, "there was a Japanese screen in five panels, all done in gold. And a long vertical scroll with pictures of ducks and geese. And a wood sculpture of a deer, almost life-size, and very old, judging from its condition. And a big china bowl. And a gold Buddha about three feet high."

From under the table Hames said, "This guy's

fur feels like mink. Are these cats very expensive?"

It was Wojcik who roused the neighbors. The apartment across the hall was occupied by an elderly woman who was hard of hearing; she said she had retired early, had heard nothing, had seen no one. The adjoining apartment to the east was vacant; the one on the other side produced a fragment of information.

"We're not acquainted with Mr. Lyke," said a man's voice, "but we see him on the elevator occasionally—him and his friends."

"And we hear his wild parties," a woman's shrill voice added.

"We didn't hear anything tonight," said the man, "except his television. That struck us as being unusual. Ordinarily he plays stereo. . . . Music, you know."

"He doesn't play it. He *blasts* it," the woman said. "Last week we complained to the manager."

"When we heard his TV," the man went on, "we decided there must be a good show, so we turned our set on. After that I didn't hear anything more from his apartment."

"No voices? No altercation of any kind?" the detective asked.

"To tell the truth, I fell asleep," said the man. "It wasn't a very good show after all."

Wojcik nodded to the woman. "And you?"

"With the TV going and my husband snoring, who could hear a bomb go off?"

When Wojcik returned, he said to Qwilleran, "How well did you know the decedent?"

"I met him for the first time a couple of weeks ago—on assignment for the *Fluxion*. Don't know much about him except that he gave big parties, and he seemed to be well liked—by both men and women."

The detective said, "He was a decorator, hmmm?"

"Yes," said Qwilleran crisply, "and a damn good one."

"When was the last time you saw him?"

"This afternoon, when we photographed the apartment. Bunsen and I invited him to dinner at the Press Club, but he said he had a date."

"Any idea who it was?"

"No, he just said he had a date."

"Did he live alone?"

"Yes. That is, I presume he lived alone."

"What do you mean by that?"

"There's only one name on his mailbox."

"Any help working here?"

"At parties he had two people working in the kitchen and serving. The building management supplies cleaning service."

"Know any of his relatives or close friends?"

"Just his partner at the decorating studio. Better try Starkweather."

By that time the coroner's man and the police photographer had arrived, and Wojcik said to the newsmen, "Why don't you two pack up and clear out?"

"I'd like to get the doctor's statement," said Qwilleran, "so I can file a complete story."

Wojcik gave him a close look. "Aren't you the *Fluxion* man who was involved in the Tait burglary?"

"I wasn't *involved* in it," said Qwilleran. "I just happened to write a story about Mr. and Mrs. Tait's house—a few days before their houseboy made off with their jades, if one can believe the statement made by the Police Department."

From the dining room Hames called out: "Have you noticed? This cat's eyes turn red in the dark."

After a while Wojcik said to the newsmen: "Death caused by a bullet wound in the chest. Fired at close range. About ten o'clock. Weapon missing. Robbery apparently no motive. . . . That's all. Now, do us a favor and go home. You probably know more than we do. I think your paper goes around setting these things up."

To retrieve Koko, Qwilleran had to crawl under the dining table and forcibly remove the cat, who seemed to have taken root.

Hames walked the newsmen to the door. "Your Sunday supplement looks good," he said. "All those elegant homes! My wife says I should scare up a little graft so we can live like that."

"I think the magazine's a good idea," Qwilleran

said, "but it's been rough going. First the Tait setback, and then—"

"Come on, clear out!" snapped Wojcik. "We've got work to do."

"Say!" said Hames. "My wife sure liked those four-poster beds you photographed on Merchant Street. Do you know where I could buy something like that?"

Qwilleran looked distressed. "That was another unfortunate coincidence! I wish I knew why the Vice Squad picked that particular weekend to raid the place."

"Well," said Hames, "I don't know how it happened, but I know the Police Widows' Fund just received a sizable donation from the Penniman Foundation. . . . Now, what did you say was missing? Five-panel gold-leaf screen? Three-foot gold Buddha? Kakemono with ducks and geese? Antique wood carving of deer? Porcelain bowl? Are you sure it was a five-panel screen? Japanese screens usually have an even number of panels."

Slowly and thoughtfully the newsmen returned to 15-F, Bunsen carrying his camera, Qwilleran carrying the cat on his shoulder.

"The Penniman Foundation!" he repeated.

"You know who the Pennimans are, don't you?" said Bunsen.

"Yes, I know who they are. They live in Muggy Swamp. And they own the *Morning Rampage*."

FIFTEEN

Qwilleran phoned in the details of David Lyke's murder to a *Fluxion* rewrite man, and Bunsen called his wife. "Is the party over, honey? . . . Tell the girls I'll be right there to kiss 'em all good night. . . . Nothing. Not a thing. Just sat around and talked all evening. . . . Honey, you know I wouldn't do anything like that!"

The photographer left the Villa Verandah to return to Happy View Woods, and Qwilleran began to worry about Koko's prolonged tranquillity. Was the cat demonstrating feline sangfroid or had he gone into shock? Upon returning to the apartment, he should have prowled the premises, inspected the kitchen for accidental leftovers, curled up on his blue cushion on top of the refrigerator. Instead, he huddled on the bare wood floor beneath the desk, with eyes wide, looking at nothing. His attitude suggested that he was cold. Qwilleran covered him with his old corduroy sports coat, arranging it like a tent over the cat, and received no acknowledgement—not even the tremor of an ear.

Qwilleran himself was exhausted after the scare of Koko's disappearance, Bunsen's hair-raising performance, and the discovery of Lyke's body. But when he went to bed, he could not sleep. The questions followed him from side to side as he tossed.

Question: Who would want to eliminate the easygoing, openhanded David Lyke? He was equally gracious to men and women, young and old, clients and competitors, the help in the kitchen and the guests in the living room. True, he spoke out of the other side of his mouth when their backs were turned, but still he charmed them all.

Question: Could the motive be jealousy? Lyke had everything—looks, talent, personality, success, friends. He had had a date that night. Perhaps the woman had been followed by a jealous friend or a jealous husband. Or—there was another possibility—perhaps the date had not been with a woman.

Question: Why was Lyke wearing an important ring and no other apparel, except a dressing gown? And why had the bedcover been removed and neatly folded in the middle of the evening? Qwilleran frowned and blew into his moustache.

Question: Why had the neighbors heard no commotion and no shot? Perhaps the audio on Lyke's television had been turned up to full volume purposely, before the shot was fired. And the neighbors had attributed everything they heard to a television program. Wonderful invention, television.

Question: Where had Koko been during the whole episode? What had he seen? What had he done? Why did he now appear to be stunned?"

Qwilleran tossed from his left side to his right for the hundredth time. It was dawn before he finally fell asleep, and then he dreamed of telephone bells. Readers were phoning him with unanswerable questions. *Brrrring!* "What colors do you mix to get sky-blue-pink?" *Brrrring!* "Where can I buy a Danish chair made in Japan?" And the managing editor, too. *Brrrring!* "Qwill, this is Harold. We're going to carpet the Press Room. What do you think about Bourbon Brown?"

When the ringing telephone finally dragged Qwilleran from his confused sleep, he said a mindless "Hello" into the mouthpiece.

The voice at the other end said, simply, "Starkweather," and then waited.

"Yes?" said Qwilleran, groping for words. "How are you?"

"Isn't it—isn't it terrible?" said Lyke's partner. "I haven't slept all night."

Yesterday's events came tumbling back into Qwilleran's mind. "It was a shock," he agreed. "I don't understand it."

"Is there anything—I mean—could you . . ." There was a prolonged pause.

"Can I do anything for you, Mr. Starkweather?"

"Well, I thought—if you could find out what—what they're going to say in the paper . . ."

"I reported the item myself," said Qwilleran. "I phoned it in last night—just the bare facts based on the coroner's report and the detective's statement. It'll be in the first edition this morning. If there's to be any follow-up story, the editor will probably call me in. . . . Why are you concerned?"

"Well, I wouldn't want—I wouldn't like anything to reflect—you know what I mean."

"Reflect on the studio, you mean?"

"Some of our customers, you know—they're very—"

"You're afraid the papers will make it too sensational? Is that what you're trying to say? I don't know about the *Morning Rampage,* Mr. Starkweather. But you don't need to worry about the *Fluxion.* Besides, I don't know what anyone could say that would be damaging to the studio."

"Well, you know—David and his parties—his friends. He had a lot of—you know how these young bachelors are."

Qwilleran was now fully awake. "Do you have any idea of a possible motive?"

"I can't imagine."

"Jealousy, maybe?"

"I don't know."

"Do you think it had anything to do with David's Oriental art collection?"

"I just don't know," said Starkweather in his helpless tone of voice.

Qwilleran persisted. "Do you know his collection well enough to determine if anything is missing?"

"That's what the police wanted to know last night."

"Were you able to help them?"

"I went over there right away—over to David's apartment."

"What did you find?"

"Some of his best things were locked up in a closet. I don't know why."

"I can tell you why," said Qwilleran. "Dave removed them before we took pictures yesterday."

"Oh," said Starkweather.

"Did you know we were going to take pictures of Dave's apartment?"

"Yes, he mentioned it. It slipped my mind." '

"Did he tell you he was going to remove some of the art?"

"I don't think so."

"Dave told me there were certain things he didn't want the public to know he had. Were they extremely valuable?"

Starkweather hesitated. "Some of the things were—well—"

"They weren't hot, were they?"

"What?"

"Were they stolen goods?"

"Oh, no, no! He paid plenty."

"I'm sure he did," said Qwilleran, "but I'm talking about the source of the stuff. He said, 'There are some things I shouldn't even have.' What did he mean by that?"

"Well, they were—I guess you'd say—museum pieces."

"A lot of well-heeled collectors own items of museum caliber, don't they?"

"But some of David's things were—well—I guess they should never have left the country. Japan, that is."

"I see," said Qwilleran. He thought a moment. "You mean they were ostensibly protected by the government?"

"Something like that."

"National treasures?"

"I guess that's what they call them."

"Hmm . . . Did you tell the police that, Mr. Starkweather?"

"No."

"Why not?"

"They didn't ask anything like that."

Qwilleran enjoyed a moment's glee. He could picture the brusque Wojcik interrogating the laconic Starkweather. Then he thought of one more question. "Can you think of anyone who has shown particular interest in these 'protected' items?"

"No, but I wonder . . ."

"What? What do you wonder, Mr. Starkweather?"

Lyke's partner coughed. "Is the studio liable—I mean, if there's anything illegal—could they . . ."

"I doubt it. Why don't you get some sleep, Mr. Starkweather? Why don't you take a pill and try to get some sleep?"

"Oh, no! I must go to the studio. I don't know what will happen today. This is a terrible thing, you know."

When Starkweather hung up, Qwilleran felt as if he'd had all his teeth pulled. He went into the kitchen to make some coffee, and found Koko stretched out on the refrigerator cushion. The cat was lying on his side with his head thrown back and his eyes closed. Qwilleran spoke to him, and not a whisker moved. He stroked the cat, and Koko heaved a great sigh in his sleep. His hind foot trembled.

"Dreaming?" said Qwilleran. "What do you dream about? Chicken curry? People with guns that make a loud noise? I'd sure like to know what you witnessed last night."

Koko's whiskers twitched, and he threw one paw across his eyes.

The next time the telephone rang, it interrupted Qwilleran's shaving, and he answered in a mild huff. He considered shaving a spiritual rite—part ancestor worship, part reaffirmation of gender, part declaration of respectability—and it required the utmost artistry.

"This is Cokey," said a breathless voice. "I just heard the radio announcement about David Lyke. I can't believe it."

"He was murdered, all right."

"Do you have any idea who did it?"

"How would I know?"

"Are you mad at me?" Cokey said. "You're mad at me because I suggested publishing the Allison house."

"I'm not mad," said Qwilleran, letting his voice soften a little. It occurred to him that he might want to question Cokey about a few things. "I'm shaving. I've got lather all over my face."

"Sorry I called so early."

"I'll give you a ring soon, and we'll have dinner."

"How's Koko?"

"He's fine."

After saying goodbye, Qwilleran had an idea. He wiped the lather from his face, waked Koko, and placed him on the dictionary. Koko arched his back in a tense, vibrating stretch. He turned his whiskers up, rolled his eyes down, and yawned widely, showing thirty teeth, a corrugated palate, five inches of tongue, and half his gullet.

"Okay, let's play the game," Qwilleran said, after a prolonged yawn of his own.

Koko turned around three times, then rolled

over and assumed a languid pose on the open pages of the dictionary.

"Game! Game! Play the game!" Qwilleran dug his fingernails into the pages to demonstrate.

Coyly Koko rolled over on his back and squirmed in a happy way.

"You loafer! What's the matter with you?"

The cat just narrowed his eyes and looked dreamy.

It was not until Qwilleran waved a sardine under Koko's nose that he agreed to cooperate. The game was uneventful, however: *maxillary* and *maypop, travel* and *trawlnet, scallion* and *Scandinavian.* Qwilleran had hoped for more pertinent catchwords. He had to admit, though, that a couple of them made sense. The sardine can said PRODUCT OF NORWAY.

Qwilleran hurried to the office and tackled the next issue of *Gracious Abodes,* but his mind was not on the magazine. He waited until he thought Starkweather would be at the studio, and then he telephoned Mrs. Starkweather at home.

She burst into tears. "Isn't it awful?" she cried. "My David! My dear David! Why would anyone want to do it?"

"It's hard to understand," said Qwilleran.

"He was so young. Only thirty-two, you know. And so full of life and talent. I don't know what Stark will do without him."

"Did David have enemies, Mrs. Starkweather?"

"I don't know. I just can't think. I'm so upset."

"Perhaps someone was jealous of David's success. Would anyone gain by his death?"

The tears tapered off into noisy sniffing. "Nobody would gain very much. David lived high, and he gave everything away. He didn't save a penny. Stark was always warning him."

"What will happen to David's half of the business?" Qwilleran asked in a tone as casual as he could manage.

"Oh, it will go to Stark, of course. That was the agreement. Stark put up all the money for the business. David contributed his talent. He had so much of that," she added with a whimper.

"Didn't Dave have any family?"

"Nobody. Not a living soul. I think that's why he gave so many parties. He wanted people around him, and he thought he had to buy their affection." Mrs. Starkweather heaved a breathy sigh. "But it wasn't true. People just naturally adored David."

Qwilleran bit his lip. He wanted to say: Yes, but wasn't he a cad? Didn't he say cutting things about the people who flocked around him? Don't you realize, Mrs. Starkweather, that David called you a middle-aged sot?

Instead he said, "I wonder what will happen to his Oriental art collection."

"I don't know. I really don't know." Her tone hardened. "I can think of three or four spongers who'd like to get their hands on it, though!"

"You don't know if the art is mentioned in David's will?"

"No, I don't." She thought for a moment. "I wouldn't be surprised if he left it to that young Japanese who cooks for him. It's just an idea."

"What makes you think that?"

"They were very close. David was the one who set Yushi up in the catering business. And Yushi was devoted to David. We were all devoted to David." The tears started again. "I'm glad you can't see me, Mr. Qwilleran. I look awful. I've been crying for hours! David made me feel young, and suddenly I feel so old."

Qwilleran's next call was to the studio called PLUG. He recognized the suave voice that answered.

"Bob, this is Qwilleran at the *Fluxion*," he said.

"Yes, indeed!" said Orax. "How the wires are buzzing this morning! The telephone company may declare an extra dividend."

"What have you heard about Dave's murder?"

"Nothing worth repeating, alas."

"I really called," said Qwilleran, "to ask about Yushi. Do you know if he's available for catering jobs? I'm giving a party for a guy who's getting married."

Orax said: "I'm sure Yushi will have plenty of time now that David has departed. He's listed in the phone book under Cuisine Internationale. . . . Are we going to see you at the Posthumous Pour?"

"What's that?"

"Oh, didn't you know?" said Orax. "When David wrote his will, he provided for one final cocktail bash for all his friends—at the Toledo! No weeping! Just laughter, dancing and booze until the money runs out. At the Toledo it runs out very fast."

"David was a real character," Qwilleran said. "I'd like to write a profile of him for the paper. Who were his best friends? Who could fill me in?"

Orax hummed on the line for a few seconds. "The Starkweathers, of course, and the Noytons, and *dear* Yushi, and quite a few unabashed freeloaders like myself."

"Any enemies?"

"Perhaps Jacques Boulanger, but these days it's hard to tell an enemy from a friend."

"How about the girls in his life?"

"Ah, yes, girls," said Orax. "There was Lois Avery, but she married and left town. And there was a creature with long straight hair who works for Mrs. Middy; I've forgotten her name."

"I think," said Qwilleran, "I know the one you mean."

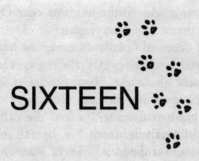

SIXTEEN

Qwilleran took a taxi to the Sorbonne Studio. He had telephoned for an appointment, and a woman with an engaging French accent had invited him to arrive *tout de suite* if he desired a *rendez-vous* with Monsieur Boulanger at the atelier.

In the taxi he thought again about Cokey. Now he knew! Koko had sensed her deception. Koko had been trying to convey that information when he nipped Cokey's head and licked the photograph from her wallet.

Qwilleran had caught only a glimpse of the picture, but he was fairly sure whose likeness the cat had licked: that arty pose, that light hair. Now he knew! Cokey—so candid, so disarming—was capable of a convincing kind of duplicity. She had allowed Qwilleran to introduce David, and the decorator had played the game with only a meager wavering of his sultry gaze. Was he playing the gentleman on a spur-of-the-moment cue? Or was there some prearranged agreement?

If Cokey had deceived Qwilleran once, she had probably deceived him twice. Had she engineered the embarrassment about the Allison house? Did she have connections at the *Morning Rampage*?

"Is this the place you want?" asked the cabdriver, rousing Qwilleran from his distasteful reverie. The taxi had stopped in front of a pretentious little building, a miniature version of the pavilions that French monarchs built for their mistresses.

The interior of the Sorbonne Studio was an awesome assemblage of creamy white marble, white carpet, white furniture, and crystal chandeliers. The carpet, thick and carved, looked like meringue. Qwilleran stepped on it cautiously.

There was an upholstered hush in the place until a dark-skinned young woman of rare beauty appeared from behind a folding screen and said, "*Bonjour, m'sieu.* May I 'elp you?"

"I have an appointment with Mr. Boulanger," said Qwilleran. "I'm from the *Daily Fluxion.*"

"*Ah, oui.* Monsieur Boulanger is on the tele-

phone with a cli*ent*, but I will announce your pre*sence*."

With a sinuous walk she disappeared behind the folding screen, which was mirrored, and Qwilleran caught a reflection of himself looking smugly appreciative at her retreating figure.

In a moment a handsome Negro, wearing a goatee, came striding out from the inner regions. "Hello, there," he said with a smile and an easy manner. "I'm Jack Baker."

"I have an appointment with Mr. Boulanger," said Qwilleran.

"I'm your man," said the decorator. "Jacques Boulanger to clients, Jack Baker to my relatives and the press. Come into my office, *s'il vous plaît.*"

Qwilleran followed him into a pale-blue room that was plush of carpet, velvety of wall, and dainty of chair. He glanced uneasily at the ceiling, entirely covered with pleated blue silk, gathered in a rosette in the center.

"*Man, I know what you're thinking.*" Baker laughed. "This is a real gone pad. *Mais malheureusement*, it's what the clients expect. Makes me feel like a jackass, but it's a living." His eyes were filled with merriment that began to put Qwilleran at ease. "How do you like the reception salon? We've just done it over."

"I guess it's all right if you like lots of white," said Qwilleran.

"Not white!" Baker gave an exaggerated shudder. "It's called Vichyssoise. It has an undertone of Leek Green."

The newsman asked: "Is this the kind of work you do for your customers? We'd like to photograph one of your interiors for *Gracious Abodes.* I understand you do a lot of interiors in Muggy Swamp."

The decorator hesitated. "I don't want to seem uncooperative, *vous savez,* but my clients don't go for that kind of publicity. And, to be perfectly frank, the designing I do in Muggy Swamp is not, *qu'est-ce qu'on dit,* newsworthy. I mean it! My clients are all squares. They like tired clichés. Preferably French clichés, and those are the worst! Now, if I could show you design with imagination and daring. Not so much taste, but more spirit."

"Too bad," said Qwilleran. "I was hoping we could get an important society name like Duxbury or Penniman."

"I wish I could oblige," said the decorator. "I really do. I dig the newspaper scene. It was an American newsman in Paris who introduced me to my first client—Mrs. Duxbury, as a matter of fact." He laughed joyously. "Would you like to hear the whole mad tale? *C'est formidable!*"

"Go ahead. Mind if I light my pipe?"

Baker began his story with obvious relish. "I was born right here in this town, on the wrong side of the wrong side of the tracks, if you know what I mean. Somehow I made college on a scholarship and came out with a Fine Arts degree, which entitled me—*ma foi!*—to work for a decorating studio, installing drapery hardware. So I saved my pennies and went to Paris, to the Sorbonne. *C'est bien ça.*" The decorator's face grew fond. "And that's where I was discovered by Mr. and Mrs. Duxbury, a couple of beautiful cats."

"Did they know you were from their own city?"

"*Mais non!* For kicks I was speaking English with a French accent, and I had grown this picturesque beard. The Duxburys bought the whole exotic bit—bless them!—and commissioned me to come here and do their thirty-room house in Muggy Swamp. I did it in tones of Oyster, Pistachio, and Apricot. After that, all the other important families wanted the Duxburys' Negro decorator from Paris. I had to continue the French accent, *vous savez.*"

"How long have you kept the secret?"

"It's no secret any longer, but it would embarrass too many people if we admitted the truth. So we all enjoy the harmless little *divertissement.* I pretend to be French, and they pretend they don't know I'm not. *C'est parfait!*" Baker grinned with pleasure as he related it.

The young lady with the ravishing face and figure walked into the office carrying a golden tray. On it were delicate teacups, slices of lemon, a golden teapot.

"This is my niece, Verna," said the decorator.

"Hi!" she said to Qwilleran. "Ready for your fix? Lemon or sugar?" There was no trace of a French accent. She was very American and very young, but she poured from the vermeil teapot with aristocratic grace.

Qwilleran said to Baker, "Who did the decorating in Muggy Swamp before you arrived on the scene?"

The decorator gave a twisted smile. "*Eh bien,* it was Lyke and Starkweather." He waited for Qwilleran's reaction, but the newsman was a veteran at hiding reactions behind his ample moustache.

"You mean you walked away with all their customers?"

"*C'est la vie.* Decorating clients are fickle. They are also sheep, especially in Muggy Swamp."

Baker was frank, so Qwilleran decided to be blunt. "How come you didn't get the G. Verning Tait account?"

The decorator looked at his niece, and she looked at him. Then Jack Baker smiled an ingratiating smile. "There was some strong feeling in the Tait family," he said, speaking carefully. "*Pourtant,* David Lyke did a good job. I would never have used that striped wallpaper in the foyer, and the lamps were out of scale, but David tried hard." His expression changed to sorrow, real or feigned. "And now I've lost my best competition. Without competition, where are the kicks in this game?"

"I'm thinking of writing a profile on David Lyke," said Qwilleran. "As a competitor of his, could you make a statement?"

"Quotable?" asked Baker with a sly look.

"How long had you know Lyke?"

"From 'way back. When we were both on the other side of the tracks. Before his name was Lyke."

"He changed his name?"

"It was unpronounceable and unspellable. Dave decided that Lyke would be more likable."

"Did you two get along?"

"*Tiens!* We were buddies in high school—a couple of esthetes in a jungle of seven-foot basketball players and teen-age goons. Secretly I felt superior to Dave because I had parents, and he was an orphan. Then I came out of college and found myself working for him—measuring windows and drilling screwholes in the woodwork so David Lyke could sell $5,000 drapery jobs and get invited to society debuts in Muggy Swamp. While I'd been grinding my brain at school and washing dishes for my keep, he'd been making it on personality and bleached hair and—who knows what else. It rankled, man; it rankled!"

Qwilleran puffed on his pipe and looked sympathetic.

"*Dites donc,* I got my revenge," Baker smiled broadly. "I came back from Paris and walked away with his Muggy Swamp clientele. And to rub it in, I moved into the same building where he lived, but in a more expensive apartment on a higher floor."

"You live at the Villa Verandah? So do I."

"Sixteenth floor, south."

"Fifteenth floor, north."

"*Alors*, we're a couple of status-seekers," said Baker.

Qwilleran had one more question. "As a competitor of David's, and a former friend, and a neighbor, do you have any educated guesses as to the motive for his murder?"

The decorator shrugged. "*Qui sait?* He was a ruthless man—in his private life as well as in business."

"I thought he was the most," said Verna.

"*Vraiment, chérie*, he had a beautiful facade, but he'd cut your throat behind your back, as the saying goes."

Qwilleran said, "I've never met anyone with more personal magnetism."

"*Eh bien!*" Baker set his jaw, and looked grim.

"Well, I'll probably see you around the mausoleum," said the newsman, as he rose to leave.

"Come up to the sixteenth floor and refuel some evening," the decorator said. "My wife's a real swinger in the kitchen."

Qwilleran went back to the office to check proofs, and he found a message to see the managing editor at once.

Percy was in a less than genial mood. "Qwill," he said abruptly, "I know you were not enthusiastic about taking the *Gracious Abodes* assignment, and I think I was wrong in pressing it on you."

"What do you mean?"

"I'm not blaming you for the succession of mishaps per se, but it does seem that the magazine has been accident-prone."

"I didn't like the idea at the beginning," said Qwilleran, "but I'm strong for it now. It's an interesting beat."

"That thing last night," said Percy, shaking his head. "That murder! Why does everything happen on your beat? Sometimes there are psychological reasons for what we call a jinx. Perhaps we should relieve you of the assignment. Anderson is retiring October first...."

"Anderson!" Qwilleran said with undisguised horror! "The church editor?"

"Perhaps you could handle church news, and *Gracious Abodes* could be turned over to the Women's Department, where it belonged in the first place."

Qwilleran's moustache reared up. "If you'd let me dig into these crimes, Harold, the way I suggested, I think I could unearth some clues. There are forces working against us! I happen to know, for example, that the Police Widows' Fund got a sizable donation from the owners of the *Morning Rampage* around the same time the Vice Squad raided the Allison house."

Percy looked weary. "They're getting one from

us, too. Every September both papers make a donation."

"All right, then. Maybe it wasn't a payoff, but I'll bet the timing wasn't accidental. And I suspect a plot in the Muggy Swamp incident, too."

"On what do you base your suspicions?"

Qwilleran smoothed his moustache. "I can't reveal my source at this time, but with further investigation—"

The editor slapped his hand on the desk with finality. "Let's leave it the way I've suggested, Qwill. You put next Sunday's magazine to bed, and then let Fran Unger take over."

"Wait! Give me one more week before you make a decision. I promise there'll be a surprising development."

"We've had nothing but surprising developments for the last fifteen days."

Qwilleran did not reply, and he did not move away from Percy's desk. He just stared the editor in the eye and waited for an affirmative—a trick he had learned from Koko.

"All right. One more week," said the editor. "And let's hope no one plants a bomb in the Press Room."

Qwilleran went back to the Feature Department with hope and doubt battling for position. He dialed the *Fluxion*'s extension at Police Headquarters and talked to Lodge Kendall. "Any news on the murder?"

"Not a thing," said the police reporter.

"They're going through Lyke's address book. It's an extensive list."

"Did they get any interesting fingerprints?"

"Not only fingerprints, but pawprints!"

"Let me know if anything breaks," Qwilleran said. "Just between you and me, my job may depend on it."

At six o'clock, as Qwilleran was leaving for dinner, he ran into Odd Bunsen at the elevator.

"Hey, do you want those photographs of the Tait house?" Bunsen said. "They've been cluttering up my locker for a week." He went back to the Photo Lab and returned with a large envelope. "I made blowups for you, same as I made for the police. What do you want them for?"

"Thought I'd give them to Tait."

"That's what I figured. I did a careful job of printing."

Qwilleran went to the Press Club, loaded a plate at the all-you-can-eat buffet, and took it to the far end of the bar, where he could eat in solitude and contemplate the day's findings: Lyke's relationship with Cokey, his unfashionable beginnings, the boyhood friendship that went sour, the national treasures that should have stayed in Japan, and the vague status of Yushi. Once during the day Qwilleran had tried to telephone Cuisine Internationale, but Yushi's answering service had said the caterer was out of town.

While the newsman was drinking his coffee, he opened the envelope. The photographs were impressive. Bunsen had enlarged them to eleven-by-fourteen and let the edges bleed. The bartender was hovering near, wiping a spot on the bar that needed no wiping, showing curiosity.

"The Tait house," Qwilleran said. "I'm going to give them to the owner."

"He'll appreciate it. People like to have pictures of their homes, their kids, their pets—anything like that." Bruno accompanied this profound observation with a sage nod.

Qwilleran said: "Did you ever hear of a cat licking glossy photos? That's what my cat does. He also eats rubber bands."

"That's not good," said the bartender. "You better do something about it."

"You think it's bad for him?"

"It isn't normal. I think your cat is, like they say, disturbed."

"He seems perfectly happy and healthy."

Bruno shook his head wisely. "That cat needs help. You should take him to a psycatatrist."

"A psyCATatrist?" said Qwilleran. "I didn't know there was such a thing."

"I can tell you where to find a good one."

"Well, thanks," said the newsman. "If I decide to take Koko to a headshrinker, I'll check back with you."

He went to the buffet for a second helping, wrapped a slice of turkey in a paper napkin, and took a taxi home to the Villa Verandah.

As soon as he stepped off the elevator on the

fifteenth floor, he started jingling his keys. It was his signal to Koko. The cat always ran to the door and raised his shrill Siamese yowl of greeting. As part of the ritual, Qwilleran would pretend to fumble with the lock, and the longer he delayed opening the door, the more vociferous the welcome.

But tonight there was no welcoming clamor. Qwilleran opened the door and quickly glanced in Koko's three favorite haunts: the northeast corner of the middle sofa; the glass-topped coffee table, a cool surface for warm days; and the third bookshelf, between a marble bust of Sappho and a copy of *Fanny Hill,* where Koko retired if the apartment was chilly. None of the three offered any evidence of cat.

Qwilleran went to the kitchen and looked on top of the refrigerator, expecting to see a round mound of light fur curled on the blue cushion— headless, tailless, legless, and asleep. There was no Koko there. He called, and there was no answer. Systematically he searched under the bed, behind the draperies, in closets and drawers, even inside the stereo cabinet. He opened the kitchen cupboards. In a moment of panic he snatched at the refrigerator door. No Koko. He looked in the oven.

All this time Koko was watching the frantic search from the seat of the green wing chair—in plain view but invisible, as a cat can be when he is silent and motionless. Qwilleran gave a grunt of surprise and relief when he finally caught sight of the hump of fur. Then he became concerned. Koko was sitting in a hunched position with his shoulder blades up and a troubled look in his eyes.

"Are you all right?" the man said.

The cat gave a mouselike squeak without opening his mouth.

"Do you feel sick?"

Koko wriggled uncomfortably and looked in the corner of the chair seat. A few inches from his nose was a ball of fluff. Green fluff.

"What's that? Where did you get that?" Qwilleran demanded. Then his eyes traveled to the wing of the chair. Across its top a patch of upholstery fabric was missing, and the padding was bursting through.

"Koko!" yelled Qwilleran. "Have you been chewing this chair? This expensive Danish chair?"

Koko gave a little cough, and produced another wad of green wool, well chewed.

Qwilleran gasped. "What will Harry Noyton say? He'll have a fit!" Then he raised his voice to a shout, "Are you the one who's been eating my ties?"

The cat looked up at the man and purred mightily.

"Don't you dare purr! You must be crazy—to eat cloth! You're out of your mind! Lord! That's all I need—one more problem!"

Koko gave another wheezing cough, and up came a bit of green wool, very damp.

Qwilleran dashed to the telephone and dialed a number.

"Connect me with the bartender," he said, and in a moment he heard the hubbub of the Press Club bar like the roar of a hurricane. "Bruno!" he shouted. "This is Qwilleran. How do I reach that doctor? That psycatatrist?"

SEVENTEEN

The morning after Koko ate a piece of the Danish chair, Qwilleran telephoned his office and told Arch Riker he had a doctor's appointment and would be late.

"Trouble?" Riker asked.

"Nothing serious," said Qwilleran. "Sort of a digestive problem."

"That's a twist! I thought you had a stomach like a billy goat."

"I have, but last night I got a big surprise."

"Better take care of it," Riker advised. "Those things can lead to something worse."

Bruno had supplied Dr. Highspight's telephone number, and when Qwilleran called, the voice of the woman who answered had to compete with the mewing and wailing of countless cats. Speaking with a folksy English accent, she told Qwilleran he could have an appointment at eleven o'clock that morning. To his surprise she said it would not be necessary to bring the patient. She gave an address on Merchant Street, and Qwilleran winced.

He prepared a tempting breakfast for Koko—jellied consommé and breast of Press Club turkey—hoping to discourage the cat's appetite for Danish furniture. He said goodbye anxiously, and took a bus to Merchant Street.

Dr. Highspight's number was two blocks from the Allison house, and it was the same type of outdated mansion. Unlike the Allison house, which was freshly painted and well landscaped, the clinic was distinctly seedy. The lawn was full of weeds. There were loose floorboards on the porch.

Qwilleran rang the doorbell with misgivings. He had never heard of a psycatatrist, and he hated the thought of being rooked by a quack. Nor did he relish being made the victim of another practical joke.

The woman who came to the door was surrounded by cats. Qwilleran counted five of them: a tiger, an orange nondescript, one chocolate brown, and two sleek black panthers. From there his glance went to the woman's runover bedroom slippers, her wrinkled stockings, the sagging hem of her housedress, and finally to her pudgy middle-aged face with its sweet smile.

"Come in, love," she said, "before the pussies run out in the road."

"My name's Qwilleran," he said. "I have an appointment with Dr. Highspight."

His nose recorded faint odors of fish and antiseptic, and his eye perused the spacious entrance hall, counting cats. They sat on the hall table, perched on several levels of the stairway, and peered inquisitively through all the doorways. A Siamese kitten with an appealing little smudged face struck a businesslike pose in a flat box of sand that occupied one corner of the foyer.

"Eee! I'm no doctor, love," said the woman. "Just a cat fancier with a bit of common sense. Would you like a cuppa? Go in the front room and make yourself comfy, and I'll light the kettle."

The living room was high-ceilinged and architecturally distinguished, but the furniture had seen better days. Qwilleran selected the overstuffed chair that seemed least likely to puncture him with a broken spring. The cats had followed him and were now inspecting his shoelaces or studying him from a safe distance. He marveled at a cat's idea of a safe distance—roughly seven feet, the length of an average adult's lunge.

"Now, love, what seems to be the bother?" asked Mrs. Highspight, seating herself in a platform rocker and picking up a wild-looking apricot cat to hold on her lap. "I was expecting a young lad. You were in such a dither when you called."

"I was concerned about my Siamese," said Qwilleran. "He's a remarkable animal, with some unusual talents—and very friendly. But lately his behavior has been strange. He's crazy about gummed envelopes, masking tape, stamps—anything like that. He licks them!"

"Eee, I like to lick envelopes myself," said Mrs. Highspight, rocking her chair vigorously and stroking the apricot cat. "It's a caution how many flavors they can think up."

"But you haven't heard the worst. He's started eating cloth! Not just chewing it—swallowing it! I thought the moths were getting into my clothes, but I've found out it's the cat. He's nibbled three good wool ties, and last night he ate a chunk out of a chair."

"Now we're onto something!" said the woman. "Is it always wool that he eats?"

"I guess so. The chair is covered with some kind of woolly material."

"It won't hurt him. If he can't digest it, he'll chuck it up."

"That's comforting to know," said Qwilleran, "but it's getting to be a problem. It was a costly chair that he ate, and it doesn't even belong to me."

"Does he do it when you're at home?"

"No, always behind my back."

"The poor puss is lonesome. Siamese cats need

company, they do, or they get a bit daft. Is he by himself all day?"

Qwilleran nodded.

"How long has he lived with you?"

"About six months. He belonged to my landlord, who was killed last March. Perhaps you remember the murder on Blenheim Place."

"Eee, that I do! I always read about murders, and that was a gory one, that was. They done him in with a carving knife. And this poor puss—was he very fond of the murdered man?"

"They were kindred spirits. Never separated."

"That's your answer, love. The poor puss has had a shock, like. And now he's lonesome."

Qwilleran found himself rising to his own defense. "The cat's very fond of me. We get along fine. He's affectionate, and I play with him once in a while."

Just then a large smoky-blue cat walked into the room and made a loud pronouncement.

"The kettle's boiling," said Mrs. Highspight. "Tommy always notifies me when the kettle's boiling. I'll fetch the tea things and be back in a jiff."

The company of cats kept their eyes on Qwilleran until the woman returned with cups and a fat brown teapot.

"And does he talk much, this puss of yours?" she asked.

"He's always yowling about one thing or another."

"His mother pushed him away when he was a

kit. That kind always talks a blue streak and needs more affection, they do. Is he neutered?"

Qwilleran nodded. "He's what my grandmother used to call a retired gentleman cat."

"There's only one thing for it. You must get him another puss for a companion."

"Keep two cats?" Qwilleran protested.

"Two's easier than one. They keep each other entertained and help wash the places that's hard to reach. If your puss has a companion, you won't have to swab his ears with cotton and boric acid."

"I didn't know I was supposed to."

"And don't bother your head about the feed bill. Two happy cats don't eat much more than one cat that's lonesome."

Qwilleran felt a tiny breath on his neck and turned to find the pretty little Siamese he had seen in the entrance hall, now perched on the back of his chair, smelling his ear.

"Tea's ready to pour," Mrs. Highspight announced. "I like a good strong cup. There's a bit of milk in the pitcher, if you've a mind."

Qwilleran accepted a thin china cup filled with a mahogany-colored brew, and noted a cat hair floating on its surface. "Do you sell cats?" he asked.

"I breed exotics and find homes for strays," said Mrs. Highspight. "What your puss needs is a nice little Siamese ladylove—spayed, of course. Not that it makes much difference. They still know which is which, and they can be very sweet together. What's the name of your puss?"

"Koko."

"Eee! Just like Gilbert and Sullivan!" Then she sang in a remarkably good voice, " 'For he's going to marry Yum *Yum*, te dum. Your anger pray bury, for all will be merry. I think you had better succumb, te dum.' "

Tommy, the big blue point, raised his head, and howled. Meanwhile, the Siamese kitten was burrowing into Qwilleran's pocket.

"Shove her off, love, if she's a bother. She's a regular hoyden. The females always take a liking to men."

Qwilleran stroked the pale fur, almost white, and the kitten purred delicately and tried to nibble his finger with four little teeth. "If I'm going to get another cat," he said, "maybe this one—"

"Eee, I couldn't let you have that one. She's special, like. But I know where there's an orphan needs a good home. Did you hear about that Mrs. Tait that died last week? There was a burglary, and it was in all the papers."

"I know a little about it," said Qwilleran.

"A sad thing, that was. Mrs. Tait had a Siamese female, and I don't fancy her husband will be keeping the poor puss."

"What makes you think so?"

"Eee, he doesn't like cats."

"How do you know all this?"

"The puss came from one of my litters, and the missus—rest her soul!—had to call on me for help. The poor puss was so nervous, wouldn't eat, wouldn't sleep. And now the poor woman's gone, and no telling what will become of the puss. . . . Let me fill your teacup, love."

She poured more of the red-black brew with its swirling garnish of tea leaves.

"And that husband of hers," she went on. "Such a one for putting on airs, but—mind this!—I had to wait a good bit for my fee. And me with all these hungry mouths to feed!"

Qwilleran's moustache was signaling to him. He said that, under the circumstances, he would consider adopting the cat. Then he tied the shoelace the cats had untied, and stood up to leave. "How much do I owe you for the consultation?"

"Would three dollars be too much for you, love?"

"I think I can swing it," he said.

"And if you want to contribute a few pennies for the cup of tea, it goes to buy a bit of a treat for the pussies. Just drop it in the marmalade crock on the hall table."

Mrs. Highspight and an entourage of waving tails accompanied Qwilleran to the door, the Siamese kitten rubbing against his ankles and touching his heart. He dropped two quarters in the marmalade jar.

"Call on me any time you need help, love," said Mrs. Highspight.

"There's one thing I forgot to mention," Qwilleran said. "A friend visited me the other evening, and Koko tried to bite her. Not a vicious attack—just a token bite. But on the head, of all places!"

"What was the lady doing?"

"Cokey wasn't doing a thing! She was minding her own business, when all of a sudden Koko sprang at her head."

"The lady's name is Cokey, is it?"

"That's what everybody calls her."

"You'll have to call her something else, love. Koko thought you were using his name. A puss is jealous of his name, he is. Very jealous."

When Qwilleran left the cattery on Merchant Street, he told himself that Mrs. Highspight's diagnosis sounded logical; the token attack on Cokey was motivated by jealousy. At the first phone booth he stopped and called the Middy studio.

On the telephone he found Cokey strangely gentle and amenable. When he suggested a dinner date, she invited him to dinner at her apartment. She said it would be only a casserole and a salad, but she promised him a surprise.

Qwilleran went back to his office and did some writing. It went well. The words flowed easily, and his two typing fingers hit all the right keys. He also answered a few letters from readers who were requesting decorating advice:

"May I use a quilted *matelassé* on a small *bergère*?"

"Is it all right to place a low credenza under a high clerestory?"

In his agreeable mood Qwilleran told them all, "Yes. Sure. Why not?"

Just before he left the office at five thirty, the Library chief called to say that the Tait clipping file had been returned, and Qwilleran picked it up on his way out of the building.

He wanted to go home and shave before going to Cokey's, and he had to feed the cat. As soon as he stepped off the elevator on the fifteenth floor, he could hear paeans of greeting, and when he entered the apartment Koko began a drunken race through the rooms. He went up over the backs of chairs and down again with a thud. He zoomed up on the stereo cabinet and skated its entire length, rounded the dining table in a blur of light fur, cleared the desk top, knocked over the waste-basket—all the while alternating a falsetto howl with a baritone growl.

"That's the spirit!" said Qwilleran. "That's what I like to see," and he wondered if the cat sensed he was getting a playmate.

Qwilleran chopped some chicken livers for Koko and sautéed them in butter, and he crumbled a small side order of Roquefort cheese. Hurriedly he cleaned up and put on his other suit and his good plaid tie. Then it was six thirty, and time to leave. For a few seconds he hesitated over the Tait file from the Library—a bulky envelope of old society notes, obsolete business news, and obituaries. His moustache pricked up, but his stomach decided the Tait file could wait until later.

EIGHTEEN

Cokey lived on the top floor of an old town house, and Qwilleran, after climbing three flights of stairs, was breathing hard when he arrived at her apartment. She opened the door, and he lost what little breath he had left.

The girl who greeted him was a stranger. She had cheekbones, temples, a jawline, and ears. Her hair, that had formerly encased her head and most of her visage like a helmet of chain mail, was now a swirling frame for her face. Qwilleran was fascinated by Cokey's long neck and graceful chinline.

"It's great!" he said. His eyes followed her as

she moved about the apartment doing domestic and unnecessary little tasks.

The furnishings were spare, with an understated Bohemian smartness; black canvas chairs, burlap curtains in the honest color of potato sacks, and painted boards supported by clay plant pots to make a bookcase. Cokey had created a festive atmosphere with lighted candles and music. There were even two white carnations leaning out of a former vinegar bottle.

Her economies registered favorably with Qwilleran. There was something about the room that looked sad and brave to a resident of the Villa Verandah. It touched him in a vulnerable spot, and for one brief moment he had a delirious urge to support this girl for life, but it passed quickly. He pressed a handkerchief to his brow and remarked about the music coming from a portable record player.

"Schubert," she said sweetly. "I've given up Hindemith. He doesn't go with my new hairdo."

For dinner she served a mixture of fish and brown rice in a sauce flecked with green. The salad was crunchy and required a great deal of chewing, retarding conversation. Later came ice cream made of yogurt and figs, sprinkled with sunflower seeds.

After dinner Cokey poured cups of herb tea (she said it was her own blend of alfalfa and bladder wrack) and urged her guest to take the most comfortable chair and prop his feet on a hassock that she had made from a beer crate, upholstering it with shaggy carpet samples. While he lighted his pipe, she curled up on the couch—an awning-striped mattress on legs—and started knitting something pink.

"What's that?" Qwilleran gasped, and almost inhaled the match he intended to blow out.

"A sweater," she said. "I knit all my own sweaters. Do you like the color? Pink is going to be part of my new image, since I had no luck with the old image."

Qwilleran smoked his pipe and marveled at the omnipotence of hairdressers. Billions are spent for neurophysiological research to control human behavior, he reflected. Beauty shops would be cheaper.

For a while he watched the angular grace of Cokey's hands as she manipulated the knitting needles, and suddenly he said: "Tell me honestly, Cokey. Did you know the nature of the Allison house when you suggested publishing it?"

"Honestly, I didn't," she said.

"Did you happen to mention it to that fellow from the *Morning Rampage*?"

"What fellow?"

"Mike Bulmer in their Circulation Department. You seem to know him. You spoke to him at the Press Club."

"Oh, *that* one! I don't really know him. He bought some lamps from Mrs. Middy last spring and gave her a bad check; that's why I remembered him."

Qwilleran felt relieved. "I thought you were keeping secrets from me."

Cokey stopped knitting. She sighed. "There's one secret I'd better confess, because you'll find out sooner or later. You're so snoopy!"

"Occupational disease," said Qwilleran. He lighted his pipe again, and Cokey watched intently as he knocked it on the ashtray, drew on it, peered into it, filled it, tamped it, and applied a match.

"Well," said Cokey, when that was done, "it's about David Lyke. When you took me to his party and introduced him, I pretended we had never met."

"But you had," said Qwilleran. "In fact, you carry his picture in your handbag."

"How did you know?"

"You spilled everything on my sofa Saturday night, and Koko selected Lyke's picture and started licking it."

"You and your psychic cat are a good team!"

"Then it's true?"

She shrugged helplessly. "I was one of the hordes of women who fell for that man. Those bedroom eyes! And that voice like a roll of drums! . . . Of course, it never amounted to anything. David charmed everyone and loved no one."

"But you still carry his picture."

Cokey pressed her lips together, and her eyelashes fluttered. "I tore it up—a few days ago." Then all at once it became necessary for her to repair her lipstick, change the records, snuff the candles on the dinner table, put the butter in the refrigerator. When she had finished her frantic activity, she sat down again with her knitting. "Let's talk about you," she said to Qwilleran. "Why do you always wear red plaid ties?"

He fingered his neckwear tenderly. "I like them. This one is a Mackintosh tartan. I had a Bruce and a MacGregor, too, but Koko ate them."

"*Ate* them!"

"I was blaming the moths, but Koko was the culprit. I'm glad he didn't get this one. It's my favorite. My mother was a Mackintosh."

"I never heard of a cat eating ties."

"Wool-eating is a neurotic symptom," Qwilleran said with authority. "The question is: Why didn't he touch the Mackintosh? He had plenty of opportunity. He ruined all the others. Why did he spare my favorite tie?"

"He must be a very considerate cat. Has he eaten anything else?"

Qwilleran nodded gloomily. "You know that Danish Modern chair in my apartment? He ate a piece of that, too."

"It's wool," Cokey said. "Animal matter. Maybe it tastes good to neurotic cats."

"The whole apartment is full of animal matter: vicuña chairs, suede sofas, goat-hair rug! But

Koko had to pick Harry Noyton's favorite chair. How much will I have to pay to get it reupholstered?"

"Mrs. Middy will do it at cost," said Cokey, "but we'll have to order the fabric from Denmark. And how can you be sure Koko won't nibble it again?"

Qwilleran told her about Mrs. Highspight and the plan to adopt the Tait cat. "She told me Tait is unfond of cats. She also said he's slow to pay his bills."

"The richer they are, the harder it is to collect," said Cokey.

"But is Tait as rich as people think? David hinted that the decorating bill was unpaid. And when we discussed the possibility of publishing the Tait house, David said he thought he could use persuasion; it sounded as if he had some kind of leverage he could employ. Actually, Tait agreed quite readily. Why? Because he was really broke and inclined to cooperate with his creditor? Or for some other obscure reason?" Qwilleran touched his moustache. "Sometimes I think the Muggy Swamp episode is a frame-up. And I still think the police theory about the houseboy is all wet."

"Then what's happened to him?"

"Either he's in Mexico," said Qwilleran, "or he's been murdered. And if he's in Mexico, either he went of his own accord or he was sent there by the conspirators. And if he was sent, either he has the jades with him or he's clean. And if he has the jades, I'll bet you ten to one that Tait is planning a trip to Mexico in the near future. He's going away for a rest. If he heads west, he'll probably wind up in Mexico."

"You can also go west by heading east," said Cokey.

Qwilleran reached over and patted her hand. "Smart girl."

"Do you think he'd trust the houseboy with the jades?"

"You've got a point. Maybe Paolo didn't take the loot. Maybe he was dispatched to Mexico as a decoy. If that's the case, where are the jades hidden?"

The answer was a large silence filling the room. Qwilleran clicked his pipe on his teeth. Cokey clicked her knitting needles. The record player clicked as another disc dropped on the turntable. Now it was Brahms.

Finally Qwilleran said, "You know that game Koko and I play with the dictionary?" He proceeded with circumspection. "Lately Koko's been turning up some words that have significance. . . . I shouldn't talk about it. It's too incredible."

"You know how I feel about cats," said Cokey. "I'll believe anything."

"The first time I noticed it was last Sunday morning. I had forgotten to fix his breakfast, and when we played the dictionary game he turned up *hungerly.*"

Cokey clapped her hands. "How clever!"

"On the next try he turned up *feed,* but I didn't catch on until he produced *meadow mouse.* Apparently he was getting desperate. I don't think he really cares for mice."

"Why, that's like a Ouija board!"

"It gives me the creeps," said Qwilleran. "Ever since the mystery in Muggy Swamp, he's been flushing out words that point to G. Verning Tait, like *bald* and *sacroiliac.* He picked *sacroiliac* twice in one game, and that's quite a coincidence in a dictionary with three thousand pages."

"Is Mr. Tait bald?"

"Not a hair on his head. He also suffers from a back ailment. . . . Do you know what a koolo-kamba is?"

Cokey shook her head.

"It's an ape with a bald head and black hands. Koko dredged that one up, too."

"Black hands! That's poetic symbolism," Cokey said. "Can you think of any more?"

"Not every word pertains to the situation. Sometimes it's *visceripericardial* or *calorifacient.* But one day he found two significant words on one page: *rubeola* and *ruddiness.* Tait has a florid complexion, I might add."

"Oh, Qwill, that cat's really tuned in!" Cokey said. "I'm sure he's on the right track. Can you do anything about it?"

"Hardly." Qwilleran looked dejected. "I can't go to the police and tell them my cat suspects the scion of a fine old family. . . . Still, there's another possibility. . . ."

"What's that?"

"It may be," said Qwilleran, "that the police suspect Tait, too, and they're publishing the houseboy theory as a cover-up."

NINETEEN

Qwilleran arrived home from Cokey's apartment earlier than he had expected. Cokey had chased him out. She said they both had to work the next day, and she had to fix her hair and iron a blouse.

When he arrived at the Villa Verandah, Koko greeted him with a table-hopping routine that ended on the desk. The red light on the telephone was glowing. The phone had been ringing, Koko seemed to be saying, and no one had been there to answer.

Qwilleran dialed the switchboard.

"Mr. Bunsen called you at nine o'clock," the operator told him. "He said to call him at home if you came in before one A.M."

Qwilleran consulted his watch. It was not yet midnight, and he started to dial Bunsen's number. Then he changed his mind. He decided Cokey was right about the importance of image. He decided it would not hurt to enhance his own image—the enviable one of a bachelor carousing until the small hours of the morning.

Qwilleran emptied his coat pockets, draped his coat on a chairback, and sat down at the desk to browse through the Tait file of newspaper clippings. Koko watched, lounging on the desk top in a classic pose known to lions and tigers, curving his tail around a Swedish crystal paperweight.

The newsprint was in varying shades of yellow and brown, depending on the age of the news item. Each was rubber-stamped with the date of publication. It was hardly necessary to read the stamp; outmoded typefaces, as well as mellowed paper, gave a clue to the date.

First Qwilleran shuffled through the clippings hastily, hoping to spot a lurid headline. Finding none in a cursory search, he started to read systematically: three generations of Tait history in chronological disorder.

Five years ago Tait had given a talk at a meeting of the Lapidary Society. Eleven years ago his father had died. There was a lengthy feature on the Tait Manufacturing Company, apparently one of a series on family-owned firms of long standing; organized in 1883 for the manufacture of buggy whips, the company was now producing car radio antennas. Old society clippings showed the elder Taits at the opera or charity functions. Three years ago G. Verning Tait announced his intention of manufacturing antennas that looked like buggy whips. A year later a news item stated that the Tait plant had closed and bankruptcy proceedings were being instituted.

Then there was the wedding announcement of twenty-four years ago. Mr. George Verning Tait, the son of Mr. and Mrs. Verning H. Tait of Muggy Swamp, was taking a bride. The entire Tait family had gone to Europe for the ceremony. The nuptials had been celebrated at the home of the bride's parents, the Victor Thorvaldsons of—

Qwilleran's eyes popped when he read it. "The Victor Thorvaldsons of Aarhus, Denmark."

He leaned back in his chair and exhaled into his moustache.

"Koko," he said, "what do you suppose Harry Noyton is pulling off in Aarhus?"

The cat opened his mouth to reply, but there was not enough breath behind his comment to make it audible.

Qwilleran's watch said one o'clock, and he hurried through the rest of the clippings until he found what he was looking for. Then he dialed Odd Bunsen's number excitedly.

"Hope I didn't get you out of bed," he said to the photographer.

"How was your date, you old tomcat?" Bunsen demanded.

"Not bad. Not bad."

"What were you doing on Merchant Street this morning?"

"How do you know I was on Merchant Street?"

"Aha! I saw you waiting for a bus on the southwest corner of Merchant and State at eleven fifty-five."

"You don't miss a thing, do you?" Qwilleran said. "Why didn't you stop and give me a lift?"

"I was going in the other direction. Brother! You were getting an early start. It wasn't even lunchtime."

"I had a doctor's appointment."

"On Merchant Street? Ho ho HO! Ho ho HO!"

"Is that all you called about? You're a nosy old woman."

"Nope. I've got some information for you."

"I've got some news for you, too," said Qwilleran. "I've found the skeleton in the Tait closet."

"What is it?"

"A court trial. G. Verning Tait was involved in a paternity suit!"

"Ho ho HO! That old goat! Who was the gal?"

"One of the Taits' servants. She got a settlement, too. According to these old clippings it must have been a sensational trial."

"A thing like that can be a rough experience."

"You'd think a family with the Taits' money and position would settle out of court—at any cost," Qwilleran said. "I covered a paternity trial in Chicago several years ago, and the testimony got plenty raw. . . . Now, what's on *your* mind? What's this information you've got for me?"

"Nothing much," said Bunsen, "but if you're going to send those photographs to Tait, you'd better make it snappy. He's leaving the country in a couple of days."

"How do you know?"

"I ran into Lodge Kendall at the Press Club. Tait's leaving Saturday morning."

"For Mexico?" asked Qwilleran as his moustache sprang to attention.

"Nope. Nothing as obvious as that! You'd like it if he was heading for Mexico, wouldn't you?" the photographer teased.

"Well, where is he going?"

"Denmark!"

Qwilleran waked easily the next morning after a night of silly dreams that he was glad to terminate. In one episode he dreamed he was flying to Aarhus to be best man at the high-society wedding of two neutered cats.

Before leaving for the office, he telephoned Tait and offered to deliver the photographs of the jade the next day. He also inquired about the female cat and was appalled to hear that Tait had put her out of the house to fend for herself.

"Can you get her back?" Qwilleran asked, controlling his temper. He had a particular loathing for people who mistreated animals.

"She's still on the grounds," Tait said. "She howled all night. I'll let her come back in the house. . . . How many photos do you have for me?"

Qwilleran worked hard and fast at the office that day, while the clerk in the Feature Department intercepted all phone calls and uninvited visitors with the simple explanation that permits no appeal, no argument, no exceptions. "Sorry, he's on deadline."

Only once did he take time out, and that was to telephone the Taits' former housekeeper.

"Mrs. Hawkins," he said, taming his voice to an aloof drawl, "this is an acquaintance of Mr. Tait in Muggy Swamp. I am being married shortly, and my wife and I will need a housekeeper. Mr. Tait recommends you highly—"

"Oh, he does, does he?" said a musical voice with impudence in the inflection.

"Could you come for an interview this evening at the Villa Verandah?"

"Who'll be there? Just you? Or will the lady be there?"

"My fiancée is unfortunately in Tokyo at the

moment, and it will be up to me to make the arrangements."

"Okey doke. I'll come. What time?"

Qwilleran set the appointment for eight o'-clock. He was glad he was not in need of a house-keeper. He wondered if Mrs. Hawkins was an example of Tait's ill-advised economies.

By the time Mrs. Hawkins presented herself for the interview, the rain had started, and she arrived with dripping umbrella and a dripping raincoat over a gaudy pink and green dress. Qwilleran noted that the dress had the kind of neckline that slips off the shoulder at the slightest encourage-ment, and there was a slit in the side seam. The woman had sassy eyes, and she flirted her shoul-ders when she walked. He liked sassy, flirtatious females if they were young and attractive, but Mrs. Hawkins was neither.

With exaggerated decorum he offered her a glass of sherry "against the weather," and poured a deep amber potion from Harry Noyton's well-stocked bar. He poured an exceptionally large glass, and by the time the routine matters had been covered—experience, references, salary—Mrs. Hawkins had relaxed in the cushions of a suede sofa and was ready for a chatty evening.

"You're one of the newspaper fellows that came to the house to take pictures," she an-nounced at this point, with her eyes dancing at him. "I remember your moustache." She waved an arm at the appointments of the room. "I didn't know reporters made so much money."

"Let me fill your glass," said Qwilleran.

"Aren't you drinking?"

"Ulcers," he said with a look of self-pity.

"Lordy, I know all about *them*!" said Mrs. Hawkins. "I cooked for two people with ulcers in Muggy Swamp. Sometimes, when Mr. Tait wasn't around, *she* would have me fix her a big plate of French fried onion rings, and if there's anything that doesn't go with ulcers, it's French fried onion rings, but I never argued. Nobody dared argue with her. Everybody went around on tippy-toe, and when she rang that bell, everybody dropped everything and rushed to see what she wanted. But I didn't mind, because—if I have my druthers—I druther cook for a couple of invalids than a houseful of hungry brats. And I had help out there. Paulie was a big help. He was a sweet boy, and it's too bad he turned out to be no good, but that's the way it is with foreigners. I don't understand foreigners. *She* was a foreigner, too, although it was a long time ago that she came over here, and it wasn't until near the end that she started screaming at all of us in a foreign language. Screaming at her husband, too. Lordy, that man had the patience of a saint! Of course, he had his workshop to keep him happy. He was crazy about those rocks! He bought a whole mountain once—some place in South America. It was supposed to be chock-full of jade, but I guess it didn't pan out. Once he offered me a big jade brooch, but I wouldn't take it. I wasn't having any of *that*!" Mrs. Hawkins rolled her eyes suggestively. "He was all excited when you came to take pictures of his knickknacks, which surprised me because of the way he felt about the *Daily Fluxion*." She paused to drain her glass. "This is good! One more little slug? And then I'll be staggering home."

"How did Mr. Tait feel about the *Fluxion*?" Qwilleran asked casually, as he refilled Mrs. Hawkins's glass.

"Oh, he was dead set against it! Wouldn't have it in the house. And that was a crying shame, because everybody knows the *Fluxion* has the best comics, but . . . that's the way he was! I guess we all have our pecu—peculiarities. . . . Whee! I guess I'm feeling these drinks."

Eventually she lapsed into a discourse on her former husband and her recent surgery for varicose veins. At that point Qwilleran said he would let her know about the housekeeping position, and he marched her to a taxi and gave her a five-dollar bill to cover the fare.

He returned to the apartment just as Koko emerged from some secret hiding place. The cat was stepping carefully and looking around with cautious eye and incredulous ears.

"I feel the same way," Qwilleran said. "Let's play the game and see if you can come up with something useful."

They went to the dictionary, and Koko played brilliantly. Inning after inning he had Qwilleran stumped with *ebionitism* and *echidna, cytodiagnosis* and *czestochowa, onychophore* and *opalinid*.

Just as Qwilleran was about to throw in the sponge, his luck changed. Koko sank his claws into the front of the book, and the page opened to *arene* and *argue*. On the very next try it was *quality* and *quarreled*. Qwilleran felt a significant vibration in his moustache.

TWENTY

The morning after Mrs. Hawkins's visit and Koko's stellar performance with the dictionary, Qwilleran waked before the alarm clock rang, and bounded out of bed. The pieces of the puzzle were starting to fall into place.

Tait must have had a grudge against the *Fluxion* ever since the coverage of the paternity trial. The family had probably tried to hush it up, but the *Fluxion* would naturally insist that the public has a right to know. None of the agonizing details had been spared. Perhaps the *Rampage* had dealt more kindly with the Taits; it was owned by the

Pennimans, who were part of the Muggy Swamp clique.

For eighteen years Tait had lived with his grudge, letting it grow into an obsession. Despite his subdued exterior, he was a man of strong passions. He probably hated the *Fluxion* as fervently as he loved jade. His ulcers were evidence of inner turmoil. And when the *Fluxion* offered to publish his house, he saw an opportunity for revenge; he could fake a theft, hide the jades, and let them be recovered after the newspaper had simmered in its embarrassment.

What would be a safe hiding place for a teapot as thin as a rose petal? Qwilleran asked himself as he prepared Koko's breakfast.

But would Tait go to such lengths for the meager satisfaction of revenge? He would need a stronger motive. Perhaps he was not so rich as his position indicated. He had lost the manufacturing plant; he had gambled on a jade expedition that failed to produce; he owed a large decorating bill. Had he devised a scheme to collect insurance? Had he and his wife argued about it? Had they quarreled on the night of the alleged theft? Had the quarrel been violent enough to cause a fatal heart attack?

Qwilleran placed Koko's breakfast on the kitchen floor, slipped into his suit coat, and started filling his pockets. Here and there around the apartment he collected his pipe, tobacco pouch, matches, card case, a comb, some loose silver, his bill clip, and a clean handkerchief, but he could not find the green jade button that usually rattled around in his change pocket. He remembered leaving it on the desk top.

"Koko, did you steal my lucky piece?" Qwilleran said.

"YARGLE!" came the reply from the kitchen, a yowl gargled with a throatful of veal kidneys in cream.

Once more Qwilleran opened the envelope of photographs he was going to deliver to Tait. He spread them on the desk: wide-angle pictures of beautiful rooms, medium shots of expensive furniture groupings, and close-ups of the jades. There was a perfect shot of the rare white teapot as well as one of the bird perched on the back of a lion. There were the black writing desk, ebony and black marble heavily ornamented with gilded bronze; the table supported by a sphinx; the white silk chairs that did not look comfortable.

Koko rubbed against Qwilleran's ankles.

"What's on your mind?" the man said. "I made your breakfast. Go and finish it. You've hardly touched that food!"

The cat arched his back, curved his tail into a question mark, and walked back and forth over the newsman's shoes.

"You're getting your playmate today," Qwilleran said. "A little cross-eyed lady cat. Maybe I should take you along. Would you like to put on your harness and go for a ride?"

Koko pranced in figure eights with long-legged grace.

"First I've got to punch another hole in your harness."

The kitchen offered no tools for punching holes in leather straps: no awl, no icepick, no sixpenny nails, not even an old-fashioned can opener. Qwilleran managed the operation with the point of a nail file.

"There!" he said, as he went to look for Koko. "I defy you to slip out of it again! . . . Now, where the devil did you go?"

There was a wet, slurping, scratching sound, and Qwilleran wheeled around. Koko was on the desk. He was licking a photograph.

"Hey!" yelled Qwilleran, and Koko jumped to the floor and bounded away like a rabbit.

The newsman examined the prints. Only one of them was damaged. "Bad cat!" he said. "You've blistered this beautiful photo."

Koko sat under the coffee table, hunched in a small bundle.

It was the Biedermeier armoire he had licked with his sandpaper tongue. The surface of the photograph was still sticky. From one angle the damage was hardly noticeable. Only when the light hit the picture in a certain way could the dull and faintly blistered patch be noticed.

Qwilleran examined it closely and marveled at the detail in Bunsen's photo. The grain of the wood stood out clearly, and whatever lighting the photographer had used gave the furniture a three-dimensional quality. The chased metal around the tiny keyhole was in bold relief. A fine line of shadow accentuated the edge of the drawer across the bottom.

There was another thin dark line down the side panel of the armoire that Qwilleran had not noticed before. It sliced through the grain of the wood. It hardly made sense in the design or construction of the cabinet.

Qwilleran felt a prickling in his moustache, and stroked it hurriedly. Then he grabbed Koko and trussed him in his harness.

"Let's go," he said. "You've licked something that gives me ideas!"

It was a long and expensive taxi ride to Muggy Swamp. Qwilleran listened to the click of the meter and wondered if he could put this trip on his expense account. The cat sat on the seat close to the man's thigh, but as soon as the taxi turned into the Tait driveway, Koko was alerted. He rose on his hind legs, placed his front paws on the window and scolded the landscape.

Qwilleran told the driver, "I want you to wait and take me back to town. I'll probably be a half hour."

"Okay if I go to the railway station and get some breakfast?" the man asked. "I'll stop the meter."

Qwilleran tucked the cat under his left arm, coiled the leash in his left hand, and rang the

doorbell of the Spanish mansion. As he stood
waiting, he detected a note of neglect about the
premises. The grass was badly in need of cutting.
Curled yellow leaves, the first of the season to
fall, were swirling around the courtyard. The windows were muddied.

When the door opened, it was a changed man
who stood there. Tait, despite his high color,
looked strained and tired. The old clothes and
tennis shoes he wore were in absurd contrast to
the black-and-white marble elegance of the foyer.
Muddied footprints had dried on the white marble squares.

"Come in," said Tait. "I was just packing some
things away." He made an apologetic gesture toward his garb.

"I brought Koko along," said Qwilleran coolly.
"I thought he might help in finding the other
cat." And he thought, Something's gone wrong,
or he's scared or the police have been questioning
him. Have they linked the murder of his decorator with the theft of his jades?

Tait said, "The other cat's here. It's locked up in
the laundry room."

Koko squirmed, and was transferred to Qwilleran's shoulder, where he could survey the scene.
The cat's body was taut, and Qwilleran could feel
a vibration like a low-voltage electric current.

He handed the envelope of photographs to Tait
and accepted an offhand invitation into the living
room. It had changed considerably. The white silk

chairs were shrouded with dust covers. The draperies were drawn across the windows. And the jade cases were dark and empty.

One lamp was lighted in the shadowy room—a lamp on the writing desk, where Tait had apparently been working. A ledger lay open there, and his collection of utilitarian jades was scattered over the desk—the primitive scrapers, chisels, and ax heads.

Tait yanked a dust cover off a deskside chair and motioned Qwilleran to sit down, while he himself stood behind the desk and opened the envelope. The newsman glanced at the ledger upside down; it was a catalog of the jade collection, written in a precise, slanted hand.

While the jade collector studied the photographs, Qwilleran studied the man's face. This is not the look of grief, he thought; this is exhaustion. The man has not been sleeping well. His plan is not working out.

Tait shuffled through the photographs, crimping the corners of his mouth and breathing heavily.

"Pretty good photography, isn't it?" said Qwilleran.

"Yes," Tait murmured.

"Surprising detail."

"I didn't realize he had taken so many pictures."

"We always take more than we know we can use."

Qwilleran cast a side-glance at the armoire. There was no fine dark line down the side of the cabinet—at least, none that could be discerned from where he sat.

Tait said, "This desk photographed well."

"It has a lot of contrast. Too bad there's no picture of the Biedermeier wardrobe." He watched Tait closely. "I don't know what happened. I was sure Bunsen had photographed the wardrobe."

Tait maneuvered the corners of his mouth. "It's a fine piece. It belonged to my grandfather."

Koko squirmed again and voiced a small protest, and the newsman stood up, strolled back and forth and patted the silky back. He said: "This is the first time this cat has gone visiting. I'm surprised he's so well behaved." He walked close to the armoire, and still he could see no fine dark line.

"Thank you for the pictures," Tait said. "I'll go and get the other cat."

When the collector left the room, Qwilleran's curiosity came to a boil. He walked to the armoire and examined the side panel. There was indeed a crack running vertically from top to bottom, but it was virtually invisible. Qwilleran ran his finger along the line. It was easier to feel than to see. Only the camera with its uncanny vision had observed clearly the hairline joining.

Koko was struggling now, and Qwilleran placed him on the floor, keeping the leash in his hand. Experimentally he ran his free hand up and down the crevice. He thought, It *must* be a concealed compartment. It's got to be! But how does it open? There was no visible hardware of any kind.

He glanced toward the foyer, listened for approaching footsteps, then applied himself to the puzzle. Was it a touch latch? Did they have touch latches in the old days? The cabinet was over a hundred years old.

He pressed the side panel and thought that it had a slight amount of give, as if it were less than solid. He pressed again, and it responded with a tiny cracking noise like the sound of old, dry wood. He pressed the panel hard along the edge of the crack—first at shoulder level, then higher, then lower. He reached up and pressed it at the top, and the side of the armoire slowly opened with a labored groan.

It opened only an inch or two. Cautiously Qwilleran increased the opening enough to see what was inside. His lips formed a silent exclamation. For a moment he was transfixed. He felt a prickle in his blood, and he forgot to listen for footsteps. Koko's ears were pivoting in alarm. Tennis shoes were coming noiselessly down the corridor, but Qwilleran didn't hear. He didn't see Tait enter the room . . . stop abruptly . . . move swiftly. He heard only the piercing soprano scream, and then it was too late.

The scene blurred in front of his eyes. But he saw the spike. He heard the snarls and blood-chilling shrieks. There was a shock of white lightning. The lamp crashed. In the darkness he saw the uplifted spike . . . saw the spiraling white blur . . . felt the tug at his hand . . . heard the great wrenching thud . . . felt the sharp pain . . . felt the trickle of blood . . . and heard a sound like escaping steam. Then all else was still.

Qwilleran leaned against the armoire and looked down. Blood was dripping from his fingertips. The leash was cutting into his other palm, and twelve feet of nylon cord were wound tightly around the legs of G. Verning Tait, who lay gasping on the floor. Koko, anchored at the other end of the leash, was squirming to slip out of his harness. The room was silent except for the hard breathing of the prisoner and the hissing of a female cat on top of the Biedermeier armoire.

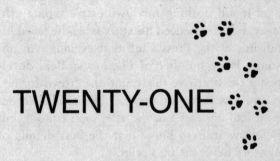

TWENTY-ONE

The nurse in the First Aid room at the *Fluxion* bandaged the slash on Qwilleran's hand.

"I'm afraid you'll live," she said cheerfully. "It's only a scratch."

"It bled a lot," he said. "That spike was razor-sharp and a foot long! It was actually a jade harpoon used for spearing walrus in the Arctic."

"How appropriate—under the circumstances," said the nurse with an affectionate side-glance at Qwilleran's moustache.

"Lucky I didn't get it in the stomach!"

"The wound looks clean," said the nurse, "but if it gives you any trouble, see a doctor."

"You can skip the commercial," Qwilleran said. "I know it by heart."

She patted the final strip of adhesive tape, and admired her handiwork.

The nurse had made a good show of the bandage. It did nothing for Qwilleran's typing efficiency, but it enhanced his story when he faced his audience at the Press Club that evening. An unusually large number of *Fluxion* staffers developed a thirst at five thirty, and the crowd formed around Qwilleran at the bar. His published account had appeared in the afternoon edition, but his fellow staffers knew that the best details of any story never get into print.

Qwilleran said, with barely suppressed pride: "It was Koko who alerted me to the hoax. He licked one of Bunsen's photos and drew attention to the secret compartment."

"I used sidelighting," Bunsen explained. "I put a light to the left of the camera at a ninety-degree angle, and it showed up the tiny crack. The camera caught it, but the eye would never know it was there."

"When I discovered the swing-out compartment packed full of jade," said Qwilleran, "I was so fascinated that I didn't hear Tait coming. First thing I knew, a cat shrieked, and there was that guy coming at me with an Eskimo harpoon, a spike *this long*!" He measured an exaggerated twelve inches with his hands. "Koko was snarling. The other cat was flying around, screaming. And there was that maniac, coming at me with a spike! Everything went out of focus. Then—crash! Tait fell flat on his face." Qwilleran displayed his bandaged hand. "He must have hurled the spike as he fell."

Arch Riker said, "Tell them how your cat tripped him up."

Qwilleran took time to light his pipe, while his audience waited for the inside story: "Koko was on a long leash, and he flew around in circles so fast—all I could see was a smoke ring in midair. And when Tait crashed to the floor, his legs were neatly trussed up in twelve feet of cord."

"Crazy!" said the photographer. "Wish I'd been there with a movie camera."

"I picked up the jade spike and kept Tait down on the floor while I called the police on that gold-plated French phone."

"When you go, you go first class," Bunsen said.

Then Lodge Kendall arrived from Headquarters. "Qwill was right all along," he told everyone. "The houseboy was innocent. Tait has told the police that he staked Paolo to a one-way fare to Mexico, then transferred the jade to the wardrobe cabinet and threw one piece behind Paolo's bed. And you remember the missing luggage? He'd given it to the boy himself."

"Was it the insurance money he was after?"

"Chiefly. Tait wasn't an astute businessman.

He'd lost the family fortune, and he needed a large sum of cash to invest in another harebrained scheme. . . . But there was something else, too. He hates the *Fluxion*. Ever since they played up his role in a paternity case."

"I'd like to know why he didn't settle that claim out of court," Qwilleran said.

"He tried, but he was up against dirty politics, he claims. It seems there was another Tait, a cousin of George Verning, who was running for Congress that year, and the paternity claim was timed accordingly. Somebody figured the voters wouldn't know one Tait from another, and apparently it was true. The guy lost the election."

Qwilleran said, "Did Tait tell the police anything about his proposed trip to Denmark?"

"Nobody mentioned it at Headquarters."

"Well," said Riker, "I'll tune in tomorrow for the next installment. I'm going home to dinner."

"I'm going home to feed Koko a filet mignon," said Qwilleran. "After all, he saved my neck."

"Don't kid yourself," Bunsen said. "He was chasing that female cat."

"I dropped her off at the pet hospital," Qwilleran said. "She had an infected wound in her side. That guy probably gave her a kick when he threw her out."

Qwilleran had floated high on excitement all afternoon, but when he arrived home he succumbed to exhaustion. Koko reacted the same way. The cat lay on his side, legs stiffly extended, one ear bent under his head—to all appearances a dead cat except for a thoughtful look in half-open eyes. He ignored his dinner.

Qwilleran went to bed early, and his dreams were pertinent and convincing. He dreamed that Percy was saying, "Qwill, you and Koko have done such a good job on the Tait case, we want you to find David Lyke's murderer," and Qwilleran said, "The investigation may take us to Japan, Chief," and Percy said, "Go right ahead! You can have an unlimited expense account." Qwilleran's moustache twitched in his sleep. So did the cat's whiskers. Koko was dreaming, too.

Early Saturday morning, while Qwilleran was snoring gently and his subconscious was wrestling with the Lyke mystery, the telephone began ringing insistently. When it succeeded in shaking him awake, he reached groggily toward the bedside table, found the receiver, and heard the operator say: "This is Aarhus, Denmark. I have a call for Mr. James Qwilleran."

"Speaking," Qwilleran croaked in his early-morning voice.

"Qwill, this is Harry," came a transatlantic shout. "We just heard the news!"

"You did? In Denmark?"

"It came over the radio."

"It's a big shame. He was a nice guy."

"I don't know about *him*," said Noyton. "I only knew her. He must have cracked up."

"Who cracked up?"

"What's the matter? Aren't you awake yet?"

"I'm awake," said Qwilleran. "What are you talking about?"

"Is this Qwill? This *is* Qwilleran, isn't it?"

"I think so. I'm a little groggy. Are you talking about the murder?"

"Murder!" shouted Noyton. "What murder?"

Qwilleran paused. "Aren't you talking about David Lyke?"

"I'm talking about G. Verning Tait! What's happened to David?"

"He's dead. He was shot last Monday night."

"David dead! My God! Who did it?"

"They don't know. It happened in his apartment. In the middle of the evening."

"Somebody break in?"

"It doesn't appear so."

"Why would anyone want to kill David? He was a fantastic guy!"

"What was it you heard on the radio over there?" Qwilleran asked.

"About Tait's arrest. Mrs. Tait's family couldn't believe it when they heard the news."

Qwilleran sat up straight. "You know her family?"

"Just met them. Fine people. Her brother's working with me on the hush-hush deal I told you about. Don't forget: I promised you the *Fluxion* will get the scoop!"

"What's the nature of it?"

"I'm financing a fantastic manufacturing

process. Qwill, I'm going to be the richest man in the world!"

"Is it a new invention?"

"A scientific discovery," Noyton said. "While the rest of the world is fooling around with outer space, the Danes are doing something for mankind here and now."

"Sounds great!"

"Until I got over here, I didn't know what it was all about. I just took her word that it was something world-shaking."

"Whose word?"

"Mrs. Tait's."

"She tipped you off to her brother's discovery?"

"Well, you see, Dr. Thorvaldson needed financing, and she knew her husband couldn't swing it. She'd heard about me and thought I could handle it. Of course, she wanted a kickback—under the table, so to speak." Noyton paused. "This is all off-the-record, of course."

Qwilleran said: "Tait was heading for Denmark. He probably expected to invest the insurance money."

There was some interference on the line.

"Are you still there?" Qwilleran said.

Noyton's voice had faded. "Listen, I'll call you tomorrow—can you hear me?—as soon as everything's sewed up legally. . . . This is a lousy connection. . . . Hope they nab David's killer. So long! Call you within twenty-four hours."

It was Saturday, but Qwilleran went into the

office to work ahead on the next issue of *Gracious Abodes*. He was determined, now, that Fran Unger should not get the magazine away from him. He hoped also to see Percy and say "I told you so," but the managing editor was attending a publishers' conference in New York. During the day Qwilleran made two important phone calls—one to the hospital to inquire about the cat, and one to the Middy Studio to make a dinner date with Cokey.

When he went home in the late afternoon to feed Koko, he found a scene of frantic activity. Koko was careening drunkenly around the apartment. He was playing with his homemade mouse—a game related to hockey, basketball, and tennis, with elements of wrestling. The cat skidded the small gray thing over the polished floor, pounced on it, tossed it in the air, batted it across the room, pursued it, made a flying tackle, clutched it in his forepaws, and rolled back and forth in ecstasy until the mouse slipped from his grasp, and the chase began again. With an audience Koko was inclined to vaunt his prowess. As Qwilleran watched, the cat dribbled the mouse the length of the living room, gave it a well-aimed whack, and scored a goal—directly under the old Spanish chest. Then he trotted after it, peered under the low chest, and raised his head in a long, demanding howl.

"No problem," said Qwilleran. "This time I'm equipped."

From the hall closet he brought the umbrella that Mrs. Hawkins had so conveniently forgotten. The first sweep under the chest produced nothing but dust, and Koko increased the volume of his demands. Qwilleran got down on the floor and poked the finial into far dark corners, fishing out the jade button that had disappeared a few days before. Koko's clamor was loud and unceasing.

The next sweep of the umbrella brought forth something pink!

Not exactly pink, Qwilleran told himself, but almost pink . . . and it looked vaguely familiar. He had an idea what it was. And he knew very well how it had managed to get there.

"Koko!" he said sternly. "What do you know about this?"

Before the cat could answer with a guttural sound and a wrestling match with an invisible enemy, Qwilleran went to the telephone and rapidly dialed a number.

"Cokey," he said, "I'm going to be late picking you up. Why don't you take a cab to the Press Club and meet me there? . . . No, just a little business emergency I've got to handle . . . All right. See you shortly. And I may have some news for you!"

Qwilleran turned back to the cat. "Koko, when did you eat this pink stuff? Where did you find it?"

When Qwilleran arrived at the Press Club, Cokey was waiting in the lobby, sitting in one of the worn leather sofas.

"There's trouble," she said. "I can read it in your face."

"Wait till we get a table, and I'll explain," he said. "Let's sit in the cocktail lounge. I'm expecting a phone call."

They went to a table with a red-checked tablecloth, well patched and darned.

"There's been an unexpected development in connection with David's murder," Qwilleran began, "and Koko's involved. He was in David's apartment when the fatal shot was fired, and he apparently ate some wool. When I brought him home that night, he looked odd. I thought he'd had a fright. Now I'm inclined to think it was a stomachache. I suppose cats get stomachaches."

"He couldn't digest the wool?" Cokey said.

"He might have managed the wool, but there was something else in the cloth. After he came home, he must have upchucked the whole thing and hidden it under the Spanish chest. I found it an hour ago."

Cokey clapped her hands to her face. "And you recognized it? Don't tell me you actually *recognized* it!"

"Yes, and I think it would have looked familiar to you, too. It was a yellowish-pink wool with gold metallic threads."

"Natalie Noyton! That handwoven dress she wore to the party!"

Qwilleran nodded. "It appears that Natalie was in Dave's apartment Monday night, and she may have been there when he was shot. At any rate, it was something that had to be reported to the police, so I took the peach-colored wool over to Headquarters. That's why I was late."

"What did they say?"

"When I left, they were hustling out to Lost Lake Hills. Our police reporter promised to call me here if anything develops."

"I wonder why Natalie didn't come forward and volunteer some information to the police?"

"That's what worries me," said Qwilleran. "If she had information to give, and the killer knew it, he might try to silence her."

The domed ceiling of the club multiplied the voices of the Saturday-night crowd into a roar, but above it came an amplified announcement on the public-address system: "Telephone for Mr. Qwilleran."

"That's our night man at Police Headquarters. I'll be right back." He hurried to the phone booth.

When he returned, his eyes had acquired a darkness.

"What's wrong, Qwill? Is it something terrible?"

"The police were too late."

"Too late?"

"Too late to find Natalie alive."

"Murdered!"

"No. She took her own life," said Qwilleran.

"Evidently a heavy dose of alcohol and then sleeping pills."

A sad wail came from Cokey. "But why? Why?"

"Apparently it was explained in her diary. She was hopelessly in love with her decorator, and he wasn't one to discourage an affair."

"That I know!"

"Natalie thought Dave was ready to marry her the moment she got a divorce, and she wanted him so desperately that she agreed to her husband's terms: no financial settlement and no request for child custody. Then last weekend it dawned on her that Dave would never marry her—or anyone else. When Odd Bunsen and I turned up at her house Monday morning and she refused to see us, she must have been out of her mind with disappointment and remorse and a kind of hopeless panic."

"I'd be blind with fury!" said Cokey.

"She was blind enough to think she could set things right by killing David."

"Then it was Natalie—"

"It was Natalie. . . . Afterward, she went home, dismissed the maid, and lived through twenty-four hours of hell before ending it. She's been dead since Tuesday night."

There was a long silence at the table.

After a while Qwilleran said, "The police found the peach-colored dress in her closet. The shawl had quite a lot of fringe missing."

Then the menus came, and Cokey said: "I'm not hungry. Let's go for a walk—and talk about other things."

They walked, and talked about Koko and the new cat whose name was Yu or Freya.

"I hope they'll be happy together," said Cokey.

"I think we're all going to be happy together," said Qwilleran. "I'm going to change her name to Yum Yum. I've got to change your name, too."

The girl looked at him dreamily.

"You see," said Qwilleran, "Koko doesn't like it when I call you Cokey. It's too close to his own name."

"Just call me Al," said Alacoque Wright with a wistful droop in her voice and a resigned lift to her eyebrows.

It was Monday when the news of Harry Noyton's Danish enterprise appeared on the front page of the *Daily Fluxion* under Qwilleran's byline. In the first edition a typographical error had substituted "devious" for "diverse," but it was a mistake so customary that the item would have been disappointing without it:

"Harry Noyton, financier and promoter of devious business interests," said the bulletin, "has acquired the worldwide franchise for a Danish scientist's unique contribution to human welfare—calorie-free beer with Vitamin C added."

On the same day, in a small ceremony at the Press Club, Qwilleran was presented with an honorary press card for his cat. On it was pasted Koko's identification photo, with eyes wide, ears alert, whiskers bristling.

"I took his picture," said Odd Bunsen, "that night in David Lyke's apartment."

And Lodge Kendall said, "Don't think I had an easy time getting the police chief and fire commissioner to sign it!"

When Qwilleran returned to the Villa Verandah that evening, he entered the apartment with his fingers crossed. He had brought Yum Yum home from the hospital at noon, and the two cats had had several hours in which to sniff each other, circle warily, and make their peace.

All was silent in the living room. On the green Danish chair sat Yum Yum, looking dainty and sweet. Her face was a poignant triangle of brown, and her eyes were enormous circles of violet-blue, slightly crossed. Her brown ears were cocked at a flirtatious angle. And where the silky hairs of her pelt grew in conflicting directions on her white breast, there was a cowlick of fur softer than down.

Koko sat on the coffee table, tall and masterful, with a ruff of fur bushed around his neck.

"You devil!" said Qwilleran. "There's nothing neurotic about you, and there never was! You knew what you were doing all the time!"

With a grunt Koko jumped down from the table and ambled over to join Yum Yum. They sat side by side in identical positions, like bookends, with both tails curled to the right, both pairs of ears worn like coronets, both pairs of eyes ignoring Qwilleran with pointed unconcern. Then Koko gave Yum Yum's face two affectionate licks and lowered his head, arching his neck gracefully. He narrowed his eyes, and they became slits of catly ecstasy as the little female recognized her cue and washed inside his ears with her long pink tongue.

Lilian Jackson Braun

The Cat Who Went Up the Creek

JOVE